... collections are intended to present the representative stories of the masters of science fiction in chronological order, their aim being to provide science fiction readers with a selection of short stories that demonstrate the authors' literary development and at the same time providing new readers with a sound introduction to their work.

The collections were compiled with the help and advice of the authors concerned, together with the invaluable assistance of numerous fans, without whose good work, time and patience they would not have been published.

In particular the advice of Roger Peyton, Gerald Bishop, Peter Weston and Leslie Flood is appreciated.

ANGUS WELLS, *Editor*, 1973

*The Best of
Arthur C. Clarke
1956–1972*

SPHERE BOOKS LIMITED
30/32 Gray's Inn Road, London, WC1X 8JL

First published in Great Britain by Sphere Books Ltd 1977
Copyright © Arthur C. Clarke 1973
Anthology copyright © Sphere Books Ltd 1973
Introduction copyright © Arthur C. Clarke 1973
Bibliography copyright © Aardvark House 1977

Originally published in one volume entitled
THE BEST OF ARTHUR C. CLARKE 1937–1971

Set in Linotype Times

Printed in Great Britain by
Hazell Watson & Viney Ltd
Aylesbury, Bucks

CONTENTS

ACKNOWLEDGMENTS

Venture to the Moon: *Fantasy & Science Fiction*, 1956
Into the Comet: *Fantasy & Science Fiction*, 1960
Summertime on Icarus: Condé Nast Publications, Inc., 1960
Death and the Senator: *Astounding Science Fiction*, 1961
Hate: *Worlds of Science Fiction*, 1961
Sunjammer: *New Worlds*, 1965
A Meeting with Medusa: Victor Gollancz Ltd, 1972

1933: A SCIENCE-FICTION ODYSSEY

by

ARTHUR C. CLARKE

WHAT makes a writer tick? One element in his composition is certainly the desire to show off. The earliest memory of my schooldays is of standing in front of the class and spinning stories about prehistoric animals. In this I must have been encouraged by the village schoolmaster, Mr. Tipper. I have been lucky with my teachers; though some were better than others, I do not remember a bad one.

When I was about nine (on the other side of the Atlantic, Goddard had just launched his first liquid-fuelled rocket ...) Mr. Tipper felt that I needed wider academic horizons than could be provided by Bishops Lydeard, population *circa* 500. So I was transferred to Huish's Grammar School, Taunton, where I received my secondary education and remained until I entered the Civil Service in 1936 at the age of nineteen.

At Huish, under the influence of the English master Captain E. B. Mitford, I began to write sketches and short stories for the School Magazine. A third of a century later I was able to repay something of my debt by dedicating 'The Nine Billion Names of God' to 'Mitty, my first editor'.

I can still recall those editorial sessions back in the early 1930s. About once a week, after class, Mitty would gather his schoolboy staff together, and we would all sit around a table on which there was a large bag of toffees. Bright ideas were rewarded instantly; Mitty invented positive reinforcement years before B. F. Skinner. He also employed a heavy metre rule for *negative* reinforcement, but this was used only in class – never, so far as I recall, at editorial conferences.

My first printed words thus appeared in the *Huish Maga-*

zine, where I eventually published at least a dozen items, totalling several thousand words. Most of these pieces were only of ephemeral interest, being full of topical allusions which not even the author can now identify. However, even in those days my science-fictional tendencies were obvious, as will be seen from the following letter from 'Ex-Sixth Former' stationed at a torrid and high-altitude Outpost of Empire: Vrying Pan, British Malaria.

It is almost impossible to keep any liquid except under enormous pressure. However, with the powerful refrigerating plant at the rubber mines here it is possible to reduce water to its boiling point, which is a great convenience to us in the hot weather.

The precautions we have to take to preserve our lives are extraordinary. Our houses are built on the principle of the Dewar vacuum flask, to keep out the heat, and the outsides are silvered to reflect the sunlight ... We have to take great care to avoid cutting ourselves in any way, for if this happens our blood soon boils and evaporates.

Electricity is very cheap here, as we can get large supplies from thermocouples. The hot end is in the sun, and the cold terminal in the boiler room at the mines, which is the coolest place in Vrying Pan ...

However, I must leave off now as my ink has evaporated, in spite of the water-cooled jacket of my fountain pen.

This effort graced the Xmas 1933 issue of the *Huish Magazine* – which, for good measure, also contains two other short pieces, heavily disguised under the pseudonym 'Clericus'. They must mark my first appearance in print.

Even in 1933, I was obviously already writing about the Moon, and I know why. I had fallen under the spell of the old science-fiction pulps, and can still recall the very first issue I ever owned. The cover of the March 1930 *Astounding Stories of Super Science*, containing Ray Cumming's 'Brigands of the Moon', is still clear and bright in my memory.

During my lunch hour I used to haunt Woolworth's, where issues of *Astounding*, *Amazing* and *Wonder* could be picked up for threepence. Much of the hard-earned money my widowed mother had saved for my food went on these magazines; I regard it as one of the best investments I ever made. I set myself the goal of obtaining a complete set of all the S.F. magazines, and had practically achieved this when the outbreak of war in 1939 caused a slight shift in priorities.

Half a lifetime later, I can still remember the ecstasy of receiving parcels – once even a *crate*! – of S.F. magazines I had bought for a few pence. Eventually I had a collection of three or four hundred magazines, which evaporated some time during the War. It would now be worth a small fortune.

The young readers of today, born into a world where many of the marvels of the 1930s have already come true, and where S.F. magazines, books and films are commonplace instead of rareties that had to be sought like gold, can scarcely imagine the impact of these old pulps. Of course, the literary standards were usually abysmal – but the stories were full of ideas, and amply evoked the famous 'sense of wonder' which is the goal of the best fiction. I see nothing incongruous in applying to those garish magazines Keats' immortal

> *Charmed magic casements, opening on the foam*
> *Of perilous sea, in faery lands forlorn.*

Soon after 1930 I came under the spell of a considerably more literate influence. In the public library at Minehead, the small West of England town where I was born, I discovered a copy of W. Olaf Stapledon's titanic *Last and First*

Men (1930). No book before or since ever had such an impact on me. The Stapledonic vistas of millions and hundreds of millions of years, the rise and fall of civilizations and entire races of men, changed my whole outlook on the universe and has influenced much of my writing ever since.

Twenty years later I was to meet Stapledon, and persuaded him to give a talk entitled 'Interplanetary Man' to the British Interplanetary Society, of which I was then chairman. His was one of the noblest and most civilized spirits I have ever encountered; I am glad that there is now a revival of interest in his work and thought.

But hard-cover books of S.F. were still very rare, and magazines were my mainstay. Through their correspondence columns I made many friends, in particular the English writer Eric Frank Russell, who encouraged my early efforts. It was thanks to Eric that I earned my first cash – as opposed to toffees – from writing. He used one of my ideas in a short story, and paid me handsomely for it. I wish I had kept his long, witty letters, written in the most beautiful hand I have ever seen. In this permissive age, most of them would now be quite printable – but, alas, they too were lost during the war years. Thank you, Eric, for your kindness to an annoyingly persistent schoolboy.

Science fiction has always encouraged an enormous amount of amateur writing, and there have been literally thousands of duplicated (sometimes printed) magazines put out by enthusiastic 'fans'. These have served a very useful purpose in providing launching pads for many professional writers in the field. The first stories I ever completed appeared in some of these magazines, and a few samples may be of interest now. If they do nothing else they may serve as a kind of absolute zero from which my later writing may be calibrated.

'The Awakening' appeared in the February 1942 issue

(No. 4) of *Zenith*, edited in Manchester by Harry Turner and Marion Eadie. A revised version was published in *Reach for Tomorrow*.

'Travel by Wire!' was published in the second issue (December 1937) of *Amateur Science Fiction Stories*, edited in Leeds by Douglas W. F. Mayer. 'Retreat From Earth' appeared in the third (and last!) issue, dated March 1938 – which also contained another story of mine, 'How We Went to Mars'.

'Whacky' appeared in *Fantast*, edited by Douglas Webster of Aberdeen, of July 1942 (Vol. 3, No. 2, whole number 14). The same issue contains my first serial, of interest only to S.F. fans: 'A Short History of Fantocracy'. I am happy to see how many of the characters therein are still active, thirty years later.

Incidentally, I have discovered with much interest that some of these ancient magazines contain perfectly dreadful pieces by a certain Ray Bradbury. I am keeping them carefully for purposes of blackmail.

Just before the War, the first British S.F. Magazine *Tales of Wonder* was put together by Walter H. Gillings. Walter did more than buy my first articles and stories – he *gave* me my first typewriter, which I carried home on a London bus from his home in Ilford. And he is the only editor I ever encountered who turned a story down, saying that it was too good for him – and a rival editor would pay more. The least I could do in gratitude was to dedicate my first collection, *Expedition to Earth*, to him.

But in spite of the traditions of Wells, Doyle, Haggard and Kipling, S.F. did not flourish in England and its spiritual home was still the United States – as in many ways it still is. I sold my first stories to John Campbell of *Astounding* (later *Analog*) during the closing months of the War, while I was in the Royal Air Force. His first purchase was 'Rescue Party' – though 'Loophole', sold a little later, actually appeared first. At the time of these sales (1945) I was stationed just outside Stratford-on-Avon, and I remember thinking modestly that there was something singularly appropriate about this.

The stories that follow were written, therefore, during a period of thirty years from 1933 to 1963. They were selected by Sphere's editor Angus Wells from my six volumes of short stories, which contain virtually everything I have written in this genre.

These tales should speak for themselves and I do not think it is appropriate to comment further on them. However, there is an historical footnote to 'Death and the Senator' which is of some interest. This story was written in 1961, long before the great days of the U.S. space programme, and foretold an era when it had fallen on hard times – as has indeed happened. And now Nature has imitated Art, for this fictional account of a U.S. space committee hearing has *itself* been read as evidence to the House of Representatives Committee on Astronautics (March 14th, 1972)! I hasten to add that though I have known all the NASA Administrators, none of them is reflected in the character of Dr. Harkness.

And I suppose everyone knows what happened to 'The Sentinel', sixteen years after I wrote it at Christmas 1948. Those who would like detailed instructions for turning a 'glittering pyramid' into a black monolith will find them in *The Lost Worlds of 2001*.

ARTHUR C. CLARKE

Colombo, Sri Lanka
December 1972

VENTURE TO THE MOON

THE story of the first lunar expedition has been written so many times that some people will doubt if there is anything fresh to be said about it. Yet all the official reports and eye-witness accounts, the on-the-spot recordings and broadcasts never, in my opinion, gave the full picture. They said a great deal about the discoveries that were made – but very little about the men who made them.

As captain of the *Endeavour* and thus commander of the British party, I was able to observe a good many things you will not find in the history books, and some – though not all – of them can now be told. One day, I hope, my opposite numbers on the *Goddard* and the *Ziolkovski* will give their points of view. But as Commander Vandenburg is still on Mars and Commander Krasnin is somewhere inside the orbit of Venus, it looks as if we will have to wait a few more years for *their* memoirs.

Confession, it is said, is good for the soul. I shall certainly feel much happier when I have told the true story behind the timing of the first lunar flight, about which there has always been a good deal of mystery.

As everyone knows, the American, Russian and British ships were assembled in the orbit of Space Station Three, five hundred miles above the Earth, from components flown up by relays of freight rockets. Though all the parts had been prefabricated, the assembly and testing of the ships took over two years, by which time a great many people – who did not realize the complexity of the task – were beginning to get slightly impatient. They had seen dozens of photos and telecasts of the three ships floating there in space beside Station Three, apparently quite complete and ready to pull away from Earth at a moment's notice. What the pictures didn't show was the careful and tedious work still in progress as thousands of pipes, wires, motors and instruments were fitted and subjected to every conceivable test.

There was no definite target date for departure; since the moon is always at approximately the same distance, you can leave for it at almost any time you like – once you are ready. It makes practically no difference, from the point of view of fuel consumption, if you blast-off at full moon or new moon or at any time in between. We were very careful to make no predictions about blast-off, though everyone was always trying to get us to fix the time. So many things can go wrong in a spaceship, and we were not going to say good-bye to Earth until we were ready down to the last detail.

I shall always remember the last commanders' conference, aboard the space station, when we all announced that we were ready. Since it was a co-operative venture, each party specializing in some particular task, it had been agreed that we should all make our landings within the same twenty-four-hour period, on the preselected site in the Mare Imbrium. The details of the journey, however, had been left to the individual commanders, presumably in the hope that we would not copy each other's mistakes.

'I'll be ready,' said Commander Vandenburg, 'to make my first dummy take-off at 0900 tomorrow. What about you, gentlemen? Shall we ask Earth Control to stand by for all three of us?'

'That's O.K. by me,' said Krasnin, who could never be convinced that his American slang was twenty years out of date.

I nodded my agreement. It was true that one bank of

fuel gauges was still misbehaving, but that didn't really matter; they would be fixed by the time the tanks were filled.

The dummy run consisted of an exact replica of a real blast-off, with everyone carrying out the job he would do when the time came for the genuine thing. We had practised, of course, in mock-ups down on Earth, but this was a perfect imitation of what would happen to us when we finally took off for the moon. All that was missing was the roar of the motors that would tell us that the voyage had begun.

We did six complete imitations of blast-off, took the ships to pieces to eliminate anything that hadn't behaved perfectly, then did six more. The *Endeavour*, the *Goddard* and the *Ziolkovski* were all in the same state of serviceability. There now only remained the job of fuelling up, and we would be ready to leave.

The suspense of those last few hours is not something I would care to go through again. The eyes of the world were upon us; departure time had now been set, with an uncertainty of only a few hours. All the final tests had been made, and we were convinced that our ships were as ready as humanly possible.

It was then that I had an urgent and secret personal radio call from a very high official indeed, and a suggestion was made which had so much authority behind it that there was little point in pretending that it wasn't an order. The first flight to the moon, I was reminded, was a co-operative venture – but think of the prestige if *we* got there first. It need only be by a couple of hours ...

I was shocked at the suggestion, and said so. By this time Vandenburg and Krasnin were good friends of mine, and we were all in this together. I made every excuse I could and said that since our flight paths had already been computed there wasn't anything that could be done about it. Each ship was making the journey by the most economical route, to conserve fuel. If we started together, we should arrive together – within seconds.

Unfortunately, someone had thought of the answer to that. Our three ships, fuelled up and with their crews standing by, would be circling Earth in a state of complete readiness for several hours before they actually pulled away from their satellite orbits and headed out to the moon. At our five-hundred-mile altitude, we took ninety-five minutes to make one circuit of the Earth, and only once every revolution would the moment be ripe to begin the voyage. If we could jump the gun by one revolution, the others would have to wait the ninety-five minutes before they could follow. And so they would land on the moon ninety-five minutes behind us ...

I won't go into the arguments, and I'm still a little ashamed that I yielded and agreed to deceive my two colleagues. We were in the shadow of Earth, in momentary eclipse, when the carefully calculated moment came. Vandenburg and Krasnin, honest fellows, thought I was going to make one more round trip with them before we all set off together. I have seldom felt a bigger heel in my life than when I pressed the firing key and felt the sudden thrust of the motors as they swept me away from my mother world.

For the next ten minutes we had no time for anything but our instruments, as we checked to see that the *Endeavour* was forging ahead along her precomputed orbit. Almost at the moment that we finally escaped from Earth and could cut the motors, we burst out of shadow into the full blaze of the sun. There would be no more night until we reached the moon, after five days of effortless and silent coasting through space.

Already Space Station Three and the two other ships must be a thousand miles behind. In eight-five more minutes Vandenburg and Krasnin would be back at the correct starting point and could take off after me, as we had all planned. But they could never overcome my lead, and I hoped they wouldn't be too mad at me when we met again on the moon.

I switched on the rear camera and looked back at the distant gleam of the space station, just emerging from the shadow of Earth. It was some moments before I realized that the *Goddard* and the *Ziolkovski* weren't still floating beside it where I'd left them ...

No; they were just half a mile away, neatly matching my velocity. I stared at them in utter disbelief for a second, before I realized that every one of us had had the same idea. 'Why, you pair of double-crossers!' I gasped. Then I began to laugh so much that it was several minutes before I dared call up a very worried Earth Control and tell them that everything had gone according to plan – though in no case was it the plan that had been originally announced ...

We were all very sheepish when we radioed each other to exchange mutual congratulations. Yet at the same time, I think everyone was secretly pleased that it had turned out this way. For the rest of the trip, we were never more than a few miles apart, and the actual landing manoeuvres were so well synchronized that our three braking jets hit the moon simultaneously.

Well, almost simultaneously. I might make something of the fact that the recorder tape shows I touched down two-fifths of a second ahead of Krasnin. But I'd better not, for Vandenburg was precisely the same amount ahead of me.

On a quarter-of-a-million-mile trip, I think you could call that a photo finish ...

We had landed early in the dawn of the long lunar day, and the slanting shadows lay all around us, extending for miles across the plain. They would slowly shorten as the sun rose higher in the sky, until at noon they would almost vanish – but noon was still five days away, as we measured time on Earth, and nightfall was seven days later still. We had almost two weeks of daylight ahead of us before the sun set and the bluely gleaming Earth became the mistress of the sky.

There was little time for exploration during those first hectic days. We had to unload the ships, grow accustomed to the alien conditions surrounding us, learn to handle our electrically powered tractors and scooters, and erect the igloos that would serve as homes, offices, and labs until the time came to leave. At a pinch, we could live in the spaceships, but it would be excessively uncomfortable and cramped. The igloos were not exactly commodious, but they were luxury after five days in space. Made of tough, flexible plastic, they were blown up like balloons, and their interiors were then partitioned into separate rooms. Air locks allowed access to the outer world, and a good deal of plumbing linked to the ships' air-purification plants kept the atmosphere breathable. Needless to say, the American igloo was the biggest one, and had come complete with everything, *including* the kitchen sink – not to mention a washing machine, which we and the Russians were always borrowing.

It was late in the 'afternoon' – about ten days after we had landed – before we were properly organized and could think about serious scientific work. The first parties made nervous little forays out into the wilderness around the base, familiarizing themselves with the territory. Of course, we

18

already possessed minutely detailed maps and photographs of the region in which we had landed, but it was surprising how misleading they could sometimes be. What had been marked as a small hill on a chart often looked like a mountain to a man toiling along in a space-suit, and apparently smooth plains were often covered knee-deep with dust, which made progress extremely slow and tedious.

These were minor difficulties, however, and the low gravity – which gave all objects only a sixth of their terrestrial weight – compensated for much. As the scientists began to accumulate their results and specimens, the radio and TV circuits with Earth became busier and busier, until they were in continuous operation. We were taking no chances; even if *we* didn't get home, the knowledge we were gathering would do so.

The first of the automatic supply rockets landed two days before sunset, precisely according to plan. We saw its braking jets flame briefly against the stars, then blast again a few seconds before touchdown. The actual landing was hidden from us, since for safety reasons the dropping ground was three miles from the base. And on the moon, three miles is well over the curve of the horizon.

When we got to the robot, it was standing slightly askew on its tripod shock absorbers, but in perfect condition. So was everything aboard it, from instruments to food. We carried the stores back to base in triumph, and had a celebration that was really rather overdue. The men had been working too hard, and could do with some relaxation.

It was quite a party; the highlight, I think, was Commander Krasnin trying to do a Cossack dance in a space-suit. Then we turned our minds to competitive sports, but found that, for obvious reasons, outdoor activities were somewhat restricted. Games like croquet or bowls would have been practical had we had the equipment; but cricket and football were definitely out. In that gravity, even a football would go half a mile if it were given a good kick – and a cricket ball would never be seen again.

Professor Trevor Williams was the first person to think of a practical lunar sport. He was our astronomer, and also one of the youngest men ever to be made a Fellow of the Royal Society, being only thirty when this ultimate accolade was conferred upon him. His work on methods of interplanetary navigation had made him world famous; less well known, however, was his skill as a toxophilite. For two years in succession he had been archery champion for Wales. I was not surprised, therefore, when I discovered him shooting at a target propped up on a pile of lunar slag.

The bow was a curious one, strung with steel control wire and shaped from a laminated plastic bar. I wondered where Trevor had got hold of it, then remembered that the robot freight rocket had now been cannibalized and bits of it were appearing in all sorts of unexpected places. The arrows, however, were the really interesting feature. To give them stability on the airless moon, where, of course, feathers would be useless, Trevor had managed to rifle them. There was a little gadget on the bow that set them spinning, like bullets, when they were fired, so that they kept on course when they left the bow.

Even with this rather makeshift equipment, it was possible to shoot a mile if one wished to. However, Trevor didn't want to waste arrows, which were not easy to make; he was more interested in seeing the sort of accuracy he could get. It was uncanny to watch the almost flat trajectory of the arrows: they seemed to be travelling parallel with the ground. If he wasn't careful, someone warned Trevor, his arrows might become lunar satellites and would hit him in the back when they completed their orbit.

The second supply rocket arrived the next day, but this time things didn't go according to plan. It made a perfect touchdown, but unfortunately the radar-controlled automatic pilot made one of those mistakes that such simple-minded machines delight in doing. It spotted the only really unclimbable hill in the neighbourhood, locked its beam on to the summit of it, and settled down there like an eagle descending upon its mountain eyrie.

Our badly needed supplies were five hundred feet above our heads, and in a few hours night would be falling. What was to be done?

About fifteen people made the same suggestion at once, and for the next few minutes there was a great scurrying about as we rounded up all the nylon line on the base. Soon there was more than a thousand yards of it coiled in neat loops at Trevor's feet while we all waited expectantly. He tied one end to his arrow, drew the bow, and aimed it experimentally straight towards the stars. The arrow rose a little more than half the height of the cliff; then the weight of the line pulled it back.

'Sorry,' said Trevor. 'I just can't make it. And don't forget – we'd have to send up some kind of grapnel as well, if we want the end to stay up there.'

There was much gloom for the next few minutes, as we watched the coils of line fall slowly back from the sky. The situation was really somewhat absurd. In our ships we had enough energy to carry us a quarter of a million miles from the moon – yet we were baffled by a puny little cliff. If we had time, we could probably find a way up to the top from the other side of the hill, but that would mean travelling several miles. It would be dangerous, and might well be impossible, during the few hours of daylight that were left.

Scientists were never baffled for long, and too many ingenious (sometimes overingenious) minds were working on the problem for it to remain unresolved. But this time it was a little more difficult, and only three people got the answer simultaneously. Trevor thought it over, then said non-committally, 'Well, it's worth trying.'

The preparations took a little while, and we were all watching anxiously as the rays of the sinking sun crept higher and higher up the sheer cliff looming above us. Even if Trevor could get a line and grapnel up there, I thought to myself, it would not be easy making the ascent while encumbered with a space-suit. I have no head for heights, and was glad that several mountaineering enthusiasts had already volunteered for the job.

At last everything was ready. The line had been carefully arranged so that it would lift from the ground with the minimum of hindrance. A light grapnel had been attached to the line a few feet behind the arrow; we hoped that it would catch in the rocks up there and wouldn't let us down – all too literally – when we put our trust in it.

This time, however, Trevor was not using a single arrow. He attached four to the line, at two-hundred-yard intervals. And I shall never forget that incongruous spectacle of the space-suited figure, gleaming in the last rays of the setting sun, as it drew its bow against the sky.

The arrow sped towards the stars, and before it had lifted more than fifty feet Trevor was already fitting the second one to his improvised bow. It raced after its predecessor, carrying the other end of the long loop that was now being hoisted into space. Almost at once the third followed, lifting its section of line – and I swear that the fourth arrow, with its section, was on the way before the first had noticeably slackened its momentum.

Now that there was no question of a single arrow lifting the entire length of line, it was not hard to reach the required altitude. The first two times the grapnel fell back; then it caught firmly somewhere up on the hidden plateau – and the first volunteer began to haul himself up the line. It was true that he weighed only about thirty pounds in this low gravity, but it was still a long way to fall.

He didn't. The stores in the freight rocket started coming

down the cliff within the next hour, and everything essential had been lowered before nightfall. I must confess, however, that my satisfaction was considerably abated when one of the engineers proudly showed me the mouth organ he had had sent from Earth. Even then I felt certain that we would all be very tired of that instrument before the long lunar night had ended . . .

But that, of course, was hardly Trevor's fault. As we walked back to the ship together, through the great pools of shadow that were flowing swiftly over the plain, he made a proposal that, I am sure, has puzzled thousands of people ever since the detailed maps of the first lunar expedition were published.

After all, it does seem a little odd that a flat and lifeless plain, broken by a single small mountain, should now be labelled on all the charts of the moon as Sherwood Forest.

GREEN FINGERS

I am very sorry, now that it's too late, that I never got to know Vladimir Surov. As I remember him, he was a quiet little man who could understand English but couldn't speak it well enough to make conversation. Even to his colleagues, I suspect he was a bit of an enigma. Whenever I went aboard the *Ziolkovski*, he would be sitting in a corner working on his notes or peering through a microscope, a man who clung to his privacy even in the tight and tiny world of a spaceship. The rest of the crew did not seem to mind his aloofness; when they spoke to him, it was clear that they regarded him with tolerant affection, as well as with respect. That was hardly surprising; the work he had done developing plants and trees that could flourish far inside the Arctic Circle had already made him the most famous botanist in Russia.

The fact that the Russian expedition had taken a botanist

to the moon had caused a good deal of amusement, though it was really no odder than the fact that there were biologists on both the British and American ships. During the years before the first lunar landing, a good deal of evidence had accumulated hinting that some form of vegetation might exist on the moon, despite its airlessness and lack of water. The president of the U.S.S.R. Academy of Science was one of the leading proponents of this theory, and being too old to make the trip himself had done the next best thing by sending Surov.

The complete absence of any such vegetation, living or fossil, in the thousand or so square miles explored by our various parties was the first big disappointment the moon had reserved for us. Even those sceptics who were quite certain that no form of life could exist on the moon would have been very glad to have been proved wrong – as of course they were, five years later, when Richard and Shannon made their astonishing discovery inside the great walled plain of Eratosthenes. But *that* revelation still lay in the future; at the time of the first landing, it seemed that Surov had come to the moon in vain.

He did not appear unduly depressed, but kept himself as busy as the rest of the crew studying soil samples and looking after a little hydroponic farm whose pressurized, transparent tubes formed a gleaming network around the *Ziolkovski*. Neither we nor the Americans had gone in for this sort of thing, having calculated that it was better to ship food from Earth than to grow it on the spot – at least until the time came to set up a permanent base. We were right in terms of economics, but wrong in terms of morale. The tiny airtight greenhouses inside which Surov grew his vegetables and dwarf fruit trees were an oasis upon which we often feasted our eyes when we had grown tired of the immense desolation surrounding us.

One of the many disadvantages of being commander was

that I seldom had much chance to do any active exploring; I was too busy preparing reports for Earth, checking stores, arranging programmes and duty rosters, conferring with my opposite numbers in the American and Russian ships, and trying – not always successfully – to guess what would go wrong next. As a result, I sometimes did not go outside the base for two or three days at a time, and it was a standing joke that my space-suit was a haven for moths.

Perhaps it is because of this that I can remember all my trips outside so vividly; certainly I can recall my only encounter with Surov. It was near noon, with the sun high above the southern mountains and the new Earth a barely visible thread of silver a few degrees away from it. Henderson, our geophysicist, wanted to take some magnetic readings at a series of check points a couple of miles to the east of the base. Everyone else was busy, and I was momentarily on top of my work, so we set off together on foot.

The journey was not long enough to merit taking one of the scooters, especially because the charges in the batteries were getting low. In any case, I always enjoyed walking out in the open on the moon. It was not merely the scenery, which even at its most awe-inspiring one can grow accustomed to after a while, No – what I never tired of was the effortless, slow-motion way in which every step took me bounding over the landscape, giving me the freedom that before the coming of space flight men only knew in dreams.

We had done the job and were halfway home when I noticed a figure moving across the plain about a mile to the south of us – not far, in fact, from the Russian base. I snapped my field glasses down inside my helmet and took a careful look at the other explorer. Even at close range, of course, you can't identify a man in a space-suit, but because the suits are always coded by colour and number that makes no practical difference.

'Who is it?' asked Henderson over the short-range radio channel to which we were both tuned.

'Blue suit, Number 3 – that would be Surov. But I don't understand. *He's by himself.*'

It is one of the most fundamental rules of lunar exploration that no one goes anywhere alone on the surface of the moon. So many accidents can happen, which would be trivial if you were with a companion – but fatal if you were by yourself. How would you manage, for example, if your space-suit developed a slow leak in the small of the back and you couldn't put on a repair patch? That may sound funny; but it's happened.

'Perhaps his buddy has had an accident and he's going to fetch help,' suggested Henderson. 'Maybe we had better call him.'

I shook my head. Surov was obviously in no hurry. He had been out on a trip of his own, and was making his leisurely way back to the *Ziolkovski*. It was no concern of mine if Commander Krasnin let his people go out on solo trips, though it seemed a deplorable practice. And if Surov was breaking regulations, it was equally no concern of mine to report him.

During the next two months, my men often spotted Surov making his lone way over the landscape, but he always avoided them if they got too near. I made some discreet inquiries, and found that Commander Krasnin had been forced, owing to shortage of men, to relax some of his safety rules. But I couldn't find out what Surov was up to, though I never dreamed that his commander was equally in the dark.

It was with an 'I told you so' feeling that I got Krasnin's emergency call. We had all had men in trouble before and had had to send out help, but this was the first time anyone had been lost and had not replied when his ship had sent out the recall signal. There was a hasty radio conference, a line of action was drawn up, and search parties fanned out from each of the three ships.

Once again I was with Henderson, and it was only common sense for us to backtrack along the route that we had seen Surov following. It was in what we regarded as 'our' territory, quite some distance away from Surov's own ship, and as we scrambled up the low foothills it occurred to me for the first time that the Russian might have been doing something he wanted to keep from his colleagues. What it might be, I could not imagine.

Henderson found him, and yelled for help over his suit radio. But it was much too late; Surov was lying, face down, his deflated suit crumpled around him. He had been kneeling when something had smashed the plastic globe of his helmet; you could see how he had pitched forward and died instantaneously.

When Commander Krasnin reached us, we were still staring at the unbelievable object that Surov had been examining when he died. It was about three feet high, a leathery greenish oval rooted to the rocks with a widespread network of tendrils. Yes – rooted; for it was a plant. A few yards away were two others, much smaller and apparently dead, since they were blackened and withered.

My first reaction was: 'So there *is* life on the moon, after all!' It was not until Krasnin's voice spoke in my ears that I realized how much more marvellous was the truth.

'Poor Vladimir!' he said. 'We knew he was a genius, yet we laughed at him when he told us of his dream. So he kept his greatest work a secret. He conquered the Arctic with his hybrid wheat, but *that* was only a beginning. He has brought life to the moon – and death as well.'

As I stood there, in that first moment of astonished revelation, it still seemed a miracle. Today, all the world knows the history of 'Surov's cactus,' as it was inevitably if quite inaccurately christened, and it has lost much of its wonder.

27

His notes have told the full story, and have described the years of experimentation that finally led him to a plant whose leathery skin would enable it to survive in vacuum, and whose far-ranging, acid-secreting roots would enable it to grow upon rocks where even lichens would be hard put to thrive. And we have seen the realization of the second stage of Surov's dream, for the cactus which will forever bear his name has already broken up vast areas of the lunar rock and so prepared a way for the more specialized plants that now feed every human being upon the moon.

Krasnin bent down beside the body of his colleague and lifted it effortlessly against the low gravity. He fingered the shattered fragments of the plastic helmet, and shook his head in perplexity.

'What could have happened to him?' he said. 'It almost looks as if the plant did it, but that's ridiculous.'

The green enigma stood there on the no-longer barren plain, tantalizing us with its promise and its mystery. Then Henderson said slowly, as if thinking aloud:

'I believe I've got the answer; I've just remembered some of the botany I did at school. If Surov designed this plant for lunar conditions, how would he arrange for it to propagate itself? The seeds would have to be scattered over a very wide area in the hope of finding suitable places to grow. There are no birds or animals here to carry them, in the way that happens on Earth. I can only think of one solution – and some of our terrestrial plants have already used it.'

He was interrupted by my yell. Something had hit with a resounding clang against the metal waistband of my suit. It did no damage, but it was so sudden and unexpected that it took me utterly by surprise.

A seed lay at my feet, about the size and shape of a plum stone. A few yards away, we found the one that had shattered Surov's helmet as he bent down. He must have known that the plant was ripe, but in his eagerness to examine it he had forgotten what that implied. I have seen a cactus throw its seed a quarter of a mile under the low lunar gravity. Surov had been shot at point-blank range by his own creation.

ALL THAT GLITTERS

This is really Commander Vandenburg's story, but he is too many millions of miles away to tell it. It concerns his geophysicist, Dr. Paynter, who was generally believed to have gone to the moon to get away from his wife.

At one time or another, we were all supposed (often by our wives) to have done just that. However, in Paynter's case, there was just enough truth to make it stick.

It was not that he disliked his wife; one could almost say the contrary. He would do anything for her, but unfortunately the things that she wanted him to do cost rather too much. She was a lady of extravagant tastes, and such ladies are advised not to marry scientists – even scientists who go to the moon.

Mrs. Paynter's weakness was for jewellery, particularly diamonds. As might be expected, this was a weakness that caused her husband a good deal of worry. Being a conscientious as well as an affectionate husband, he did not merely worry about it – he did something about it. He became one of the world's leading experts on diamonds, from the scientific rather than the commercial point of view, and probably knew more about their composition, origin, and properties than any other man alive. Unfortunately, you may know a lot about diamonds without ever possessing any, and her husband's erudition was not something that Mrs. Paynter could wear around her neck when she went to a party.

Geophysics, as I have mentioned, was Dr. Paynter's real

business; diamonds were merely a side line. He had developed many remarkable surveying instruments which could probe the interior of the Earth by means of electric impulses and magnetic waves, so giving a kind of X-ray picture of the hidden strata far below. It was hardly surprising, therefore, that he was one of the men chosen to pry into the mysterious interior of the moon.

He was quite eager to go, but it seemed to Commander Vandenburg that he was reluctant to leave Earth at this particular moment. A number of men had shown such symptoms; sometimes they were due to fears that could not be eradicated, and an otherwise promising man had to be left behind. In Paynter's case, however, the reluctance was quite impersonal. He was in the middle of a big experiment – something he had been working on all his life – and he didn't want to leave Earth until it was finished. However, the first lunar expedition could not wait for him, so he had to leave his project in the hands of his assistants. He was continually exchanging cryptic radio messages with them, to the great annoyance of the signals section of Space Station Three.

In the wonder of a new world waiting to be explored, Paynter soon forgot his earthly preoccupations. He would dash hither and yon over the lunar landscape on one of the neat little electric scooters the Americans had brought with them, carrying seismographs, magnetometers, gravity meters, and all the other esoteric tools of the geophysicist's trade. He was trying to learn, in a few weeks, what it had taken men hundreds of years to discover about their own planet. It was true that he had only a small sample of the moon's fourteen million square miles of territory to explore, but he intended to make a thorough job of it.

From time to time he continued to get messages from his colleagues back on Earth, as well as brief but affectionate signals from Mrs. P. Neither seemed to interest him very much; even when you are not so busy that you hardly have time to sleep, a quarter of a million miles puts most of your personal affairs in a different perspective. I think that on the moon Dr. Paynter was really happy for the first time in his life; if so, he was not the only one.

Not far from our base there was a rather fine crater pit, a great blowhole in the lunar surface almost two miles from rim to rim. Though it was fairly close at hand, it was outside the normal area of our joint operations, and we had been on the moon for six weeks before Paynter led a party of three men off in one of the baby tractors to have a look at it. They disappeared from radio range over the edge of the moon, but we weren't worried about that because if they ran into trouble they could always call Earth and get any message relayed back to us.

Paynter and his men were gone forty-eight hours, which is about the maximum for continuous working on the moon, even with booster drugs. At first their little expedition was quite uneventful and therefore quite unexciting; everything went according to plan. They reached the crater, inflated their pressurized igloo and unpacked their stores, took their instrument readings, and then set up a portable drill to get core samples. It was while he was waiting for the drill to bring him up a nice section of the moon that Paynter made his second great discovery. He had made his first about ten hours before, but he didn't know it yet.

Around the lip of the crater, lying where they had been thrown up by the great explosions that had convulsed the lunar landscape three hundred million years before, were immense piles of rock which must have come from many miles down in the moon's interior. Anything he could do with his little drill, thought Paynter, could hardly compare with *this*. Unfortunately, the mountain-sized geological specimens that lay all around him were not neatly arranged in their correct order; they had been scattered over the landscape, much farther than the eye could see, according to the arbitrary violence of the eruptions that had blasted them into space.

Paynter climbed over these immense slag heaps, taking a swing at likely samples with his little hammer. Presently his colleagues heard him yell, and saw him come running back to them carrying what appeared to be a lump of rather poor quality glass. It was some time before he was sufficiently coherent to explain what all the fuss was about – and some time later still before the expedition remembered its real job and got back to work.

Vandenburg watched the returning party as it headed back to the ship. The four men didn't seem as tired as one would have expected, considering the fact that they had been on their feet for two days. Indeed, there was a certain jauntiness about their movements which even the space-suits couldn't wholly conceal. You could see that the expedition had been a success. In that case, Paynter would have two causes for congratulation. The priority message that had just come from Earth was very cryptic, but it was clear that Paynter's work there – whatever it was – had finally reached a triumphant conclusion.

Commander Vandenburg almost forgot the message when he saw what Paynter was holding in his hand. He knew what a raw diamond looked like, and this was the second largest that anyone had ever seen. Only the Cullinan, tipping the scales at 3,026 carats, beat it by a slender margin. 'We ought to have expected it,' he heard Paynter babble happily. 'Diamonds are always found associated with volcanic vents. But somehow I never thought the analogy would hold here.'

Vandenburg suddenly remembered the signal, and handed it over to Paynter. He read it quickly, and his jaw dropped. Never in his life, Vandenburg told me, had he seen a man so instantly deflated by a message of congratulation. The

32

signal read: WE'VE DONE IT. TEST 541 WITH MODIFIED PRESSURE CONTAINER COMPLETE SUCCESS. NO PRACTICAL LIMIT TO SIZE. COSTS NEGLIGIBLE.

'What's the matter?' said Vandenburg, when he saw the stricken look on Paynter's face. 'It doesn't seem bad news to me, whatever it means.'

Paynter gulped two or three times like a stranded fish, then stared helplessly at the great crystal that almost filled the palm of his hand. He tossed it into the air, and it floated back in that slow-motion way everything has under lunar gravity.

Finally he found his voice.

'My lab's been working for years,' he said, 'trying to synthesize diamonds. Yesterday this thing was worth a million dollars. Today it's worth a couple of hundred. I'm not sure I'll bother to carry it back to Earth.'

Well, he *did* carry it back; it seemed a pity not to. For about three months, Mrs. P. had the finest diamond necklace in the world, worth every bit of a thousand dollars – mostly the cost of cutting and polishing. Then the Paynter Process went into commercial production, and a month later she got a divorce. The grounds were extreme mental cruelty; and I suppose you could say it was justified.

WATCH THIS SPACE

It was quite a surprise to discover, when I looked it up, that the most famous experiment we carried out while we were on the moon had its beginnings way back in 1955. At that time, high-altitude rocket research had been going for only about ten years, mostly at White Sands, New Mexico. Nineteen fifty-five was the date of one of the most spectacular of those early experiments, one that involved the ejection of sodium on to the upper atmosphere.

On Earth, even on the clearest night, the sky between the stars isn't completely dark. There's a very faint background glow, and part of it is caused by the fluorescence of sodium atoms a hundred miles up. Since it would take the sodium in a good many cubic miles of the upper atmosphere to fill a single matchbox, it seemed to the early investigators that they could make quite a fireworks display if they used a rocket to dump a few pounds of the stuff into the ionosphere.

They were right. The sodium squirted out of a rocket above White Sands early in 1955 produced a great yellow glow in the sky which was visible, like a kind of artificial moonlight, for over an hour, before the atoms dispersed. This experiment wasn't done for fun (though it *was* fun) but for a serious scientific purpose. Instruments trained on this glow were able to gather new knowledge about the upper air – knowledge that went into the stockpile of information without which space flight would never have been possible.

When they got to the moon, the Americans decided that it would be a good idea to repeat the experiment there, on a much larger scale. A few hundred kilograms of sodium fired up from the surface would produce a display that would be visible from Earth, with a good pair of field glasses, as it fluoresced its way up through the lunar atmosphere.

(Some people, by the way, still don't realize that the moon *has* an atmosphere. It's about a million times too thin to be breathable, but if you have the right instruments you can detect it. As a meteor shield, it's first-rate for though it may be tenuous it's hundreds of miles deep.)

Everyone had been talking about the experiment for days. The sodium bomb had arrived from Earth in the last supply rocket, and a very impressive piece of equipment it looked. Its operation was extremely simple; when ignited, an incendiary charge vaporized the sodium until a high pressure was built up, then a diaphragm burst and the stuff was squirted up into the sky through a specially shaped nozzle. It would be shot off soon after nightfall, and when the cloud of sodium rose out of the moon's shadow into direct sunlight it would start to glow with tremendous brilliance.

Nightfall, on the moon, is one of the most awe-inspiring sights in the whole of nature, made doubly so because as you watch the sun's flaming disc creep so slowly below the mountains you know that it will be fourteen days before you see it again. But it does not bring darkness – at least, not on this side of the moon. There is always the Earth, hanging motionless in the sky, the one heavenly body that neither rises nor sets. The light pouring back from her clouds and seas floods the lunar landscape with a soft, blue-green radiance, so that it is often easier to find your way around at night than under the fierce glare of the sun.

Even those who were not supposed to be on duty had come out to watch the experiment. The sodium bomb had been placed at the middle of the big triangle formed by the three ships, and stood upright with its nozzle pointing at the stars. Dr. Anderson, the astronomer of the American team, was testing the firing circuits, but everyone else was at a respectful distance. The bomb looked perfectly capable of living up to its name, though it was really about as dangerous as a soda-water siphon.

All the optical equipment of the three expeditions seemed to have been gathered together to record the performance. Telescopes, spectroscopes, motion-picture cameras and everything else one could think of were lined up ready for action. And this, I knew, was nothing compared with the battery that must be zeroed on us from Earth. Every amateur astronomer who could see the moon tonight would be standing by in his back garden, listening to the radio commentary that told him of the progress of the experiment.

I glanced up at the gleaming planet that dominated the sky above me; the land areas seemed to be fairly free from cloud, so the folks at home should have a good view. That seemed only fair; after all, they were footing the bill.

There were still fifteen minutes to go. Not for the first time, I wished there was a reliable way of smoking a cigarette inside a space-suit without getting the helmet so badly fogged that you couldn't see. Our scientists had solved so many much more difficult problems. It seemed a pity that they couldn't do something about that one.

To pass the time – for this was an experiment where I had nothing to do – I switched on my suit radio and listened to Dave Bolton, who was making a very good job of the commentary. Dave was our chief navigator, and a brilliant mathematician. He also had a glib tongue and a picturesque turn of speech, and sometimes his recordings had to be censored by the B.B.C. There was nothing they could do about this one, however, for it was going out live from the relay stations on Earth.

Dave had finished a brief and lucid explanation of the purpose of the experiment, describing how the cloud of glowing sodium would enable us to analyse the lunar atmosphere as it rose through it at approximately a thousand miles an hour. 'However,' he went on to tell the waiting millions on Earth, 'let's make one point clear. Even when the bomb has gone off, you won't see a darn thing for ten minutes – and neither will we. The sodium cloud will be completely invisible while it's rising up through the darkness of the moon's shadow. Then, quite suddenly, it will flash into brilliance as it enters the sun's rays, which are streaming past over our heads right now as we stare up into space. No one is quite sure how bright it will be, but it's a pretty safe guess that you'll be able to see it in any telescope bigger than a two-inch. So it should just be within the range of a good pair of binoculars.'

He had to keep this sort of thing up for another ten minutes, and it was a marvel to me how he managed to do it. Then the great moment came, and Anderson closed the firing circuit. The bomb started to cook, building up pressure inside as the sodium volatilized. After thirty seconds, there was a sudden puff of smoke from the long, slender nozzle pointing up at the sky. And then we had to wait for another ten minutes while the invisible cloud rose to the stars. After all this build-up, I told myself, the result had better be good.

The seconds and minutes ebbed away. Then a sudden yellow glow began to spread across the sky, like a vast and unwavering aurora that became brighter even as we watched. It was as if an artist was sprawling strokes across the stars with a flame-filled brush. And as I stared at those strokes, I suddenly realized that someone had brought off the greatest advertising coup in history. For the strokes formed letters, and the letters formed two words – the name of a certain soft drink too well known to need any further publicity from me.

How had it been done? The first answer was obvious. Someone had placed a suitably cut stencil in the nozzle of the sodium bomb, so that the stream of escaping vapour had shaped itself to the words. Since there was nothing to distort it, the pattern had kept its shape during its invisible ascent to the stars. I had seen skywriting on Earth, but this was something on a far larger scale. Whatever I thought of them, I couldn't help admiring the ingenuity of the men who had perpetrated the scheme. The O's and A's had given a bit of trouble, but the C's and L's were perfect.

After the initial shock, I am glad to say that the scientific programme proceeded as planned. I wish I could remember how Dave Bolton rose to the occasion in his commentary; it must have been a strain even for his quick wits. By this time, of course, half the Earth could see what he was describing. The next morning, every newspaper on the planet carried that famous photo of the crescent moon with the luminous slogan painted across its darkened sector.

The letters were visible, before they finally dispersed into space, for over an hour. By that time the words were almost a thousand miles long, and were beginning to get blurred. But they were still readable until they at last faded from sight in the ultimate vacuum between the planets.

Then the real fireworks began. Commander Vandenburg was absolutely furious, and promptly started to grill all his men. However, it was soon clear that the saboteur – if you could call him that – had been back on Earth. The bomb had been prepared there and shipped ready for immediate use. It did not take long to find, and fire, the engineer who had carried out the substitution. He couldn't have cared less, since his financial needs had been taken care of for a good many years to come.

As for the experiment itself, it was completely successful from the scientific point of view; all the recording instruments worked perfectly as they analyzed the light from the unexpectedly shaped cloud. But we never let the Americans live it down, and I am afraid poor Captain Vandenburg was the one who suffered most. Before he came to the moon he was a confirmed teetotaller, and much of his refreshment came from a certain wasp-waisted bottle. But now, as a matter of principle, he can only drink beer – and he hates the stuff.

A QUESTION OF RESIDENCE

I have already described the – shall we say – jockeying for position before take-off on the first flight to the moon. As it turned out, the American, Russian, and British ships landed just about simultaneously. No one has ever explained, however, why the British ship came back nearly two weeks after the others.

Oh, I know the official story; I ought to, for I helped to concoct it. It is true as far as it goes, but it scarcely goes far enough.

On all counts, the joint expedition had been a triumphant success. There had been only one casualty, and in the manner of his death Vladimir Surov had made himself immortal. We had gathered knowledge that would keep the scientists of Earth busy for generations, and that would revolutionize almost all our ideas concerning the nature of the universe around us. Yes, our five months on the moon had been well spent, and we could go home to such welcomes as few heroes had ever had before.

However, there was still a good deal of tidying up to be done. The instruments that had been scattered all over the lunar landscape were still busily recording, and much of the information they gathered could not be automatically radioed back to Earth. There was no point in all three of the expeditions staying on the moon to the last minute; the personnel of one would be sufficient to finish the job. But who would volunteer to be caretaker while the others went back to gain the glory? It was a difficult problem, but one that would have to be solved very soon.

As far as supplies were concerned, we had little to worry about. The automatic freight rockets could keep us provided with air, food, and water for as long as we wished to stay on the moon. We were all in good health, though a little tired. None of the anticipated psychological troubles had cropped up, perhaps because we had all been so busy on tasks of absorbing interest that we had had no time to worry about going crazy. But, of course, we all looked forward to getting back to Earth and seeing our families again.

The first change of plan was forced upon us by the *Ziolkovski* being put out of commission when the ground beneath one of her landing legs suddenly gave way. The ship managed to stay upright, but the hull was badly twisted and the pressure cabin sprang dozens of leaks. There was much debate about on-the-spot repairs, but it was decided that it would be far too risky for her to take off in this condition. The Russians had no alternative but to thumb lifts back in the *Goddard* and the *Endeavour*; by using the *Ziolkovski*'s unwanted fuel, our ships would be able to manage the extra load. However, the return flight would be extremely cramped and uncomfortable for all concerned because everyone would have to eat and sleep in shifts.

Either the American or the British ship, therefore, would be the first back to Earth. During those final weeks, as the work of the expedition was brought to its close, relations between Commander Vandenburg and myself were somewhat strained. I even wondered if we ought to settle the matter by tossing for it ...

Another problem was also engaging my attention – that of crew discipline. Perhaps this is too strong a phrase; I would not like it to be thought that a mutiny ever seemed probable. But all my men were now a little abstracted and liable to be found, if off duty, scribbling furiously in corners. I knew exactly what was going on, for I was involved in it myself. There wasn't a human being on the moon who had not sold exclusive rights to some newspaper or magazine, and we were all haunted by approaching deadlines. The radio-teletype to Earth was in continuous operation, sending tens of thousands of words a day, while even larger slabs of deathless prose were being dictated over the speech circuits.

It was Professor Williams, our very practical-minded astronomer, who came to me one day with the answer to my main problem.

'Skipper,' he said, balancing himself precariously on the all-too-collapsible table I used as my working desk inside the igloo, 'there's no technical reason, is there, why we should get back to Earth first?'

'No,' I said, 'merely a matter of fame, fortune, and seeing our families again. But I admit those aren't technical reasons. We could stay here another year if Earth kept sending supplies. If you want to suggest that, however, I shall take great pleasure in strangling you.'

'It's not as bad as that. Once the main body has gone back, whichever party is left can follow in two or three weeks at the latest. They'll get a lot of credit, in fact, for self-sacrifice, modesty, and similar virtues.'

'Which will be very poor compensation for being second home.'

'Right – we need something else to make it worth while. Some more material reward.'

'Agreed. What do you suggest?'

Williams pointed to the calendar hanging on the wall in front of me, between the two pin-ups we had stolen from the *Goddard*. The length of our stay was indicated by the days that had been crossed off in red ink; a big question mark in two weeks' time showed when the first ship would be heading back to Earth.

'There's your answer,' he said. 'If we go back then, do you realize what will happen? I'll tell you.'

He did, and I kicked myself for not having thought of it first.

The next day, I explained my decision to Vandenburg and Krasnin.

'We'll stay behind and do the mopping up,' I said. 'It's a matter of common sense. The *Goddard*'s a much bigger ship than ours and can carry an extra four people, while we can only manage two more, and even then it will be a squeeze. If you go first, Van, it will save a lot of people from eating their hearts out here for longer than necessary.'

'That's very big of you,' replied Vandenburg. 'I won't

hide the fact that we'll be happy to get home. And it's logical, I admit, now that the *Ziolkovski*'s out of action. Still, it means quite a sacrifice on your part, and I don't really like to take advantage of it.'

I gave an expansive wave.

'Think nothing of it,' I answered. 'As long as you boys don't grab all the credit, we'll take our turn. After all, we'll have the show here to ourselves when you've gone back to Earth.'

Krasnin was looking at me with a rather calculating expression, and I found it singularly difficult to return his gaze.

'I hate to sound cynical,' he said, 'but I've learned to be a little suspicious when people start doing big favours without very good reasons. And frankly, I don't think the reason you've given is good enough. You wouldn't have anything else up your sleeve, would you?'

'Oh, very well,' I sighed. 'I'd hoped to get a *little* credit but I see it's no use trying to convince anyone of the purity of my motives. I've got a reason, and you might as well know it. But please don't spread it around; I'd hate the folks back on Earth to be disillusioned. They still think of us as noble and heroic seekers after knowledge; let's keep it that way, for all our sakes.'

Then I pulled out the calendar, and explained to Vandenburg and Krasnin what Williams had already explained to me. They listened with scepticism, then with growing sympathy.

'I had no idea it was *that* bad,' said Vandenburg at last.

'Americans never have,' I said sadly. 'Anyway, that's the way it's been for half a century, and it doesn't seem to get any better. So you agree with my suggestion?'

'Of course. It suits us fine, anyhow. Until the next expedition's ready, the moon's all yours.'

I remembered that phrase, two weeks later, as I watched

the *Goddard* blast up into the sky towards the distant, beckoning Earth. It was lonely, then, when the Americans and all but two of the Russians had gone. We envied them the reception they got, and watched jealously on the TV screens their triumphant processions through Moscow and New York. Then we went back to work, and bided our time. Whenever we felt depressed, we would do little sums on bits of paper and would be instantly restored to cheerfulness.

The red crosses marched across the calendar as the short terrestrial days went by – days that seemed to have very little connexion with the slow cycle of lunar time. At last we were ready; all the instrument readings were taken, all the specimens and samples safely packed away aboard the ship. The motors roared into life, giving us for a moment the weight we would feel again when we were back in Earth's gravity. Below us the rugged lunar landscape, which we had grown to know so well, fell swiftly away; within seconds we could see no sign at all of the buildings and instruments we had so laboriously erected and which future explorers would one day use.

The homeward voyage had begun. We returned to Earth in uneventful discomfort, joined the already half-dismantled *Goddard* beside Space Station Three, and were quickly ferried down to the world we had left seven months before.

Seven months: that, as Williams had pointed out, was the all-important figure. We had been on the moon for more than half a financial year – and for all of us, it had been the most profitable year of our lives.

Sooner or later, I suppose, this interplanetary loop-hole will be plugged; the Department of Inland Revenue is still fighting a gallant rear-guard action, but we seem neatly covered under Section 57, paragraph 8 of the Capital Gains Act of 1972. We wrote our books and articles on the moon

– and until there's a lunar government to impose income tax, we're hanging on to every penny.

And if the ruling finally goes against us – well, there's always Mars ...

INTO THE COMET

'I DON'T know why I'm recording this,' said George Takeo Pickett slowly into the hovering microphone. 'There's no chance that anyone will ever hear it. They say the comet will bring us back to the neighbourhood of Earth in about two million years, when it makes its next turn around the sun. I wonder if mankind will still be in existence then, and whether the comet will put on as good a display for our descendants as it did for us? Maybe they'll launch an expedition, just as we have done, to see what they can find. And they'll find us ...

'For the ship will still be in perfect condition, even after all those ages. There'll be fuel in the tanks, maybe even plenty of air, for our food will give out first, and we'll starve before we suffocate. But I guess we won't wait for that; it will be quicker to open the air lock and get it all over.

'When I was a kid, I read a book on polar exploration called *Winter Amid the Ice*. Well, that's what we're facing now. There's ice all around us, floating in great porous bergs. *Challenger*'s in the middle of a cluster, orbiting round one another so slowly that you have to wait several minutes before you're certain they've moved. But no expedition to Earth's poles ever faced *our* winter. During most of that two million years, the temperature will be four hundred and fifty below zero. We'll be so far away from the sun that it'll give about as much heat as the stars. And who ever tried to warm his hands by Sirius on a cold winter night?'

That absurd image, coming suddenly into his mind, broke him up completely. He could not speak because of memories of moonlight upon snowfields, of Christmas chimes ringing across a land already fifty million miles away. Suddenly he was weeping like a child, his self-control dissolved by the remembrance of all the familiar, disregarded beauties of the Earth he had forever lost.

And everything had begun so well, in such a blaze of excitement and adventure. He could recall (was it only six months ago?) the very first time he had gone out to look for the comet, soon after eighteen-year-old Jimmy Randall had found it in his homemade telescope and sent his famous telegram to Mount Stromlo Observatory. In those early days, it had been only a faint polliwog of mist, moving slowly through the constellation of Eridanus, just south of the Equator. It was still far beyond Mars, sweeping sun-ward along its immensely elongated orbit. When it had last shone in the skies of Earth, there were no men to see it, and there might be none when it appeared again. The human race was seeing Randall's comet for the first and perhaps the only time.

As it approached the sun, it grew, blasting out plumes and jets, the smallest of which was larger than a hundred Earths. Like a great pennant streaming down some cosmic breeze, the comet's tail was already forty million miles long when it raced past the orbit of Mars. It was then that the astronomers realized that this might be the most spectacular sight ever to appear in the heavens; the display put on by Halley's comet, back in 1986, would be nothing in comparison. And it was then that the administrators of the International Astrophysical Decade decided to send the research ship *Challenger* chasing after it, if she could be fitted out in time; for here was a chance that might not come again in a thousand years.

For weeks on end, in the hours before dawn, the comet sprawled across the sky like a second but far brighter Milky Way. As it approached the sun, and felt again the fires it had not known since the mammoths shook the Earth, it became steadily more active. Gouts of luminous gas erupted from its core, forming great fans which turned like slowly swinging searchlights across the stars. The tail, now a hundred million miles long, divided into intricate bands and streamers which changed their patterns completely in the course of a single night. Always they pointed away from the sun, as if driven starward by a great wind blowing forever outward from the heart of the solar system.

When the *Challenger* assignment had been given to him, George Pickett could hardly believe his luck. Nothing like this had happened to any reporter since William Laurence and the atom bomb. The facts that he had a science degree, was unmarried, in good health, weighed less than one hundred and twenty pounds, and had no appendix undoubtedly helped. But there must have been many others equally qualified; well, their envy would soon turn to relief.

Because the skimpy pay load of *Challenger* could not accommodate a mere reporter, Pickett had had to double up in his spare time as executive officer. This meant, in practice, that he had to write up the log, act as captain's secretary, keep track of stores, and balance the accounts. It was very fortunate, he often thought, that one needed only three hours' sleep in every twenty-four, in the weightless world of space.

Keeping his two duties separate had required a great deal of tact. When he was not writing in his closet-sized office, or checking the thousands of items stacked away in stores, he would go on the prowl with his recorder. He had been careful, at one time or another, to interview every one of the twenty scientists and engineers who manned *Challenger*. Not all the recordings had been radioed back to Earth; some had been too technical, some too inarticulate, and others too much the reverse. But at least he had played no favourites and, as far as he knew, had trodden on no toes. Not that it mattered now.

He wondered how Dr. Martens was taking it; the astronomer had been one of his most difficult subjects, yet the one who could give most information. On a sudden impulse, Pickett located the earliest of the Martens tapes, and inserted it in the recorder. He knew that he was trying to escape from the present by retreating into the past, but the only effect of that self-knowledge was to make him hope the experiment would succeed.

He still had vivid memories of that first interview, for the weightless microphone, wavering only slightly in the draft of air from the ventilators had almost hypnotized him into incoherence. Yet no one would have guessed: his voice had its normal professional smoothness.

They had been twenty million miles behind the comet, but swiftly overtaking it, when he had trapped Martens in the observatory and thrown that opening question at him.

'Dr. Martens,' he began, 'just what *is* Randall's comet made of?'

'Quite a mixture,' the astronomer had answered, 'and it's changing all the time as we move away from the sun. But the tail's mostly ammonia, methane, carbon dioxide, water vapour, cyanogen —'

'Cyanogen? Isn't that a poison gas? What would happen if the Earth ran into it?'

'Not a thing. Though it looks so spectacular, by our normal standards a comet's tail is a pretty good vacuum. A volume as big as Earth contains about as much gas as a matchbox full of air.'

'And yet this thin stuff puts on such a wonderful display!'

'So does the equally thin gas in an electric sign, and for the same reason. A comet's tail glows because the sun bombards it with electrically charged particles. It's a cosmic sky-sign; one day, I'm afraid, the advertising people will wake up to this, and find a way of writing slogans across the solar system.'

'That's a depressing thought – though I suppose someone will claim it's a triumph of applied science. But let's leave the tail; how soon will we get into the heart of the comet – the nucleus, I believe you call it?'

'Since a stern chase always takes a long time, it will be another two weeks before we enter the nucleus. We'll be ploughing deeper and deeper into the tail, taking a cross section through the comet as we catch up with it. But though the nucleus is still twenty million miles ahead, we've already learned a good deal about it. For one thing, it's extremely small – less than fifty miles across. And even that's not solid, but probably consists of thousands of smaller bodies, all milling round in a cloud.'

'Will we be able to go into the nucleus?'

'We'll know when we get there. Maybe we'll play safe and study it through our telescopes from a few thousand miles away. But personally, I'll be disappointed unless we go right inside. Won't you?'

Pickett switched off the recorder. Yes, Martens had been right. He *would* have been disappointed, especially since there had seemed no possible source of danger. Nor was there, as far as the comet was concerned. The danger had come from within.

They had sailed through one after another of the huge but unimaginably tenuous curtains of gas that Randall's comet was still ejecting as it raced away from the sun. Yet even now, though they were approaching the densest regions of the nucleus, they were for all practical purposes in a perfect vacuum. The luminous fog that stretched around *Challenger* for so many millions of miles scarcely dimmed the stars; but directly ahead, where lay the comet's core, was a brilliant patch of hazy light, luring them onward like a will-o'-the-wisp.

The electrical disturbances now taking place around them

with ever-increasing violence had almost completely cut their link with Earth. The ship's main radio transmitter could just get a signal through, but for the last few days they had been reduced to sending 'O.K.' messages in Morse. When they broke away from the comet and headed for home, normal communication would be resumed; but now they were almost as isolated as explorers had been in the days before radio. It was inconvenient, but that was all. Indeed, Pickett rather welcomed this state of affairs; it gave him more time to get on with his clerical duties. Though *Challenger* was sailing into the heart of a comet, on a course that no captain could have dreamed of before the twentieth century, someone still had to check the provisions and count the stores.

Very slowly and cautiously, her radar probing the whole sphere of space around her, *Challenger* crept into the nucleus of the comet. And there she came to rest – amid the ice.

Back in the nineteen-forties, Fred Whipple, of Harvard, had guessed the truth, but it was hard to believe it even when the evidence was before one's eyes. The comet's relatively tiny core was a loose cluster of icebergs, drifting and turning round one another as they moved along their orbit. But unlike the bergs that floated in polar seas, they were not a dazzling white, nor were they made of water. They were a dirty grey, and very porous, like partly thawed snow. And they were riddled with pockets of methane and frozen ammonia, which erupted from time to time in gigantic gas jets as they absorbed the heat of the sun. It was a wonderful display, but Pickett had little time to admire it. Now he had far too much.

He had been doing his routine check of the ship's stores when he came face to face with disaster – though it was some time before he realized it. For the supply situation had been perfectly satisfactory; they had ample stocks for the return to Earth. He had checked that with his own eyes, and now had merely to confirm the balances recorded in the pinhead-sized section of the ship's electronic memory which stored all the accounts.

When the first crazy figures flashed on the screen, Pickett assumed that he had pressed the wrong key. He cleared the totals, and fed the information into the computer once more.

Sixty cases of pressed meat to start with; 17 consumed so far; quantity left: 99999943.

He tried again, and again, with no better result. Then, feeling annoyed but not particularly alarmed, he went in search of Dr. Martens.

He found the astronomer in the Torture Chamber – the tiny gym, squeezed between the technical stores and the bulkhead of the main propellant tank. Each member of the crew had to exercise here for an hour a day, lest his muscles waste away in this gravityless environment. Martens was wrestling with a set of powerful springs, an expression of grim determination on his face. It became much grimmer when Pickett gave his report.

A few tests on the main input board quickly told them the worst. 'The computer's insane,' said Martens. 'It can't even add or substract.'

'But surely we can fix it!'

Martens shook his head. He had lost all his usual cocky self-confidence; he looked, Pickett told himself, like an inflated rubber doll that had started to leak.

'Not even the builders could do that. It's a solid mass of microcircuits, packed as tightly as the human brain. The memory units are still operating, but the computing section's utterly useless. It just scrambles the figures you feed into it.'

'And where does that leave us?' Pickett asked.

'It means that we're all dead,' Martens answered flatly. 'Without the computer, we're done for. It's impossible to calculate an orbit back to Earth. It would take an army of mathematicians weeks to work it out on paper.'

'That's ridiculous! The ship's in perfect condition, we've plenty of food and fuel – and you tell me we're all going to die just because we can't do a few sums.'

'A *few* sums!' retorted Martens, with a trace of his old spirit. 'A major navigational change, like the one needed to break away from the comet and put us on an orbit to Earth, involves about a hundred thousand separate calculations. Even the computer needs several minutes for the job.'

Pickett was no mathematician, but he knew enough of astronautics to understand the situation. A ship coasting through space was under the influence of many bodies. The main force controlling it was the gravity of the sun, which kept all the planets firmly chained in their orbits. But the planets themselves also tugged it this way and that, though with much feebler strength. To allow for all these conflicting tugs and pulls – above all, to take advantage of them to reach a desired goal scores of millions of miles away – was a problem of fantastic complexity. He could appreciate Marten's despair; no man could work without the tools of his trade, and no trade needed more elaborate tools than this one.

Even after the Captain's announcement, and that first emergency conference when the entire crew had gathered to discuss the situation, it had taken hours for the facts to sink home. The end was still so many months away that the mind could not grasp it; they were under sentence of death, but there was no hurry about the execution. And the view was still superb ...

Beyond the glowing mists that enveloped them – and which would be their celestial monument to the end of time – they could see the great beacon of Jupiter, brighter than all the stars. Some of them might still be alive, if the others were willing to sacrifice themselves, when the ship went past the mightiest of the sun's children. Would the extra weeks of life be worth it, Pickett asked himself, to see with your own eyes the sight that Galileo had first glimpsed through his crude telescope four centuries ago – the satellites of Jupiter, shuttling back and forth like beads upon an invisible wire?

Beads upon a wire. With that thought, an all-but-forgotten childhood memory exploded out of his subconscious. It must have been there for days, struggling upward into the light. Now at last it had forced itself upon his waiting mind.

'No!' he cried aloud. 'It's ridiculous! They'll laugh at me!'

So what? said the other half of his mind. You've nothing to lose; if it does no more, it will keep everyone busy while the food and the oxygen dwindle away. Even the faintest hope is better than none at all ...

He stopped fidgeting with the recorder; the mood of maudlin self-pity was over. Releasing the elastic webbing that held him to his seat, he set off for the technical stores in search of the material he needed.

'This,' said Dr. Martens three days later, 'isn't my idea of a joke.' He gave a contemptuous glance at the flimsy structure of wire and wood that Pickett was holding in his hand.

'I guessed you'd say that,' Pickett replied, keeping his temper under control. 'But please listen to me for a minute. My grandmother was Japanese, and when I was a kid she told me a story that I'd completely forgotten until this week. I think it may save our lives.

'Sometime after the Second World War, there was a contest between an American with an electric desk calculator and a Japanese using an abacus like this. The abacus won.'

'Then it must have been a poor desk machine, or an incompetent operator.'

'They used the best in the U.S. Army. But let's stop arguing. Give me a test – say a couple of three-figure numbers to multiply.'

'Oh – 856 times 437.'

Pickett's fingers danced over the beads, sliding them up and down the wires with lightning speed. There were twelve wires in all, so that the abacus could handle numbers up to 999,999,999,999 – or could be divided into separate sections where several independent calculations could be carried out simultaneously.

'374072,' said Pickett, after an incredibly brief interval of time. 'Now see how long *you* take to do it, with pencil and paper.'

There was a much longer delay before Martens, who like most mathematicians was poor at arithmetic, called out '375072.' A hasty check soon confirmed that Martens had taken at least three times as long as Pickett to arrive at the wrong answer.

The astronomer's face was a study in mingled chagrin, astonishment, and curiosity.

'Where did you learn that trick?' he asked. 'I thought those things could only add and substract.'

'Well – multiplication's only repeated addition, isn't it? All I did was to add 856 seven times in the unit column, three times in the tens column, and four times in the hundreds column. You do the same thing when you use pencil and paper. Of course, there are some short cuts, but if you think *I'm* fast, you should have seen my granduncle. He used to work in a Yokohama bank, and you couldn't see his fingers when he was going at speed. He taught me some of the tricks, but I've forgotten most of them in the last twenty years. I've only been practising for a couple of days, so I'm still pretty slow. All the same, I hope I've convinced you that there's something in my argument.'

'You certainly have: I'm quite impressed. Can you

divide just as quickly?'

'Very nearly, when you've had enough experience.'

Martens picked up the abacus, and started flicking the beads back and forth. Then he sighed.

'Ingenious – but it doesn't really help us. Even if it's ten times as fast as a man with pencil and paper – which it isn't – the computer was a million times faster.'

'I've thought of that,' answered Pickett, a little impatiently.

(Martens had no guts – he gave up too easily. How did he think astronomers managed a hundred years ago, before there were any computers?)

'This is what I propose – tell me if you can see any flaws in it ...'

Carefully and earnestly he detailed his plan. As he did so, Martens slowly relaxed, and presently he gave the first laugh that Pickett had heard aboard *Challenger* for days.

'I want to see the skipper's face,' said the astronomer, 'when you tell him that we're all going back to the nursery to start playing with beads.'

There was scepticism at first, but it vanished swiftly when Pickett gave a few demonstrations. To men who had grown up in a world of electronics, the fact that a simple structure of wire and beads could perform such apparent miracles was a revelation. It was also a challenge, and because their lives depended upon it, they responded eagerly.

As soon as the engineering staff had built enough smoothly operating copies of Pickett's crude prototype, the classes began. It took only a few minutes to explain the basic principles; what required time was practice – hour after hour of it, until the fingers flew automatically across the wires and flicked the beads into the right positions without any need for conscious thought. There were some members of the crew who never acquired both accuracy and speed, even after a week of constant practice, but there were others who quickly out-distanced Pickett himself.

They dreamed counters and columns, and flicked beads in their sleep. As soon as they had passed beyond the elementary stage they were divided into teams, which then competed fiercely against each other, until they had reached still higher standards of proficiency. In the end, there were men aboard *Challenger* who could multiply four-figure numbers on the abacus in fifteen seconds, and keep it up hour after hour.

Such work was purely mechanical; it required skill, but no intelligence. The really difficult job was Martens', and there was little that anyone could do to help him. He had to forget all the machine-based techniques he had taken for granted, and rearrange his calculations so that they could be carried out automatically by men who had no idea of the meaning of the figures they were manipulating. He would feed them the basic data, and then they would follow the programme he had laid down. After a few hours of patient routine work, the answer would emerge from the end of the mathematical production line – provided that no mistakes had been made. And the way to guard against that was to have two independent teams working, cross-checking results at regular intervals.

'What we've done,' said Pickett into his recorder, when at last he had time to think of the audience he had never expected to speak to again, 'is to build a computer out of human beings instead of electronic circuits. It's a few thousand times slower, can't handle many digits, and gets tired easily – but it's doing the job. Not the whole job of navigating to Earth – that's far too complicated – but the simpler one of giving us an orbit that will bring us back into radio range. Once we've escaped from the electrical interference around us, we can radio our position and the big computers on Earth can tell us what to do next.

'We've already broken away from the comet and are no longer heading out of the solar system. Our new orbit checks with the calculations, to the accuracy that can be expected. We're still inside the comet's tail, but the nucleus is a million miles away and we won't see those ammonia icebergs again. They're racing on towards the stars into the freezing night between the suns, while we are coming home ...

'Hello, Earth ... hello, Earth! This is *Challenger* calling, *Challenger* calling. Signal back as soon as you receive us – we'd like you to check our arithmetic – before we work our fingers to the bone!'

SUMMERTIME ON ICARUS

WHEN Colin Sherrard opened his eyes after the crash, he could not imagine where he was. He seemed to be lying, trapped in some kind of vehicle, on the summit of a rounded hill, which sloped steeply away in all directions. Its surface was seared and blackened, as if a great fire had swept over it. Above him was a jet-black sky, crowded with stars; one of them hung like a tiny, brilliant sun low down on the horizon.

Could it be the sun? Was he so far from Earth? No – that was impossible. Some nagging memory told him that the sun was very close – hideously close – not so distant that it had shrunk to a star. And with that thought, full consciousness returned. Sherrard knew exactly where he was, and the knowledge was so terrible that he almost fainted again.

He was nearer to the sun than any man had ever been. His damaged space-pod was lying on no hill, but on the steeply curving surface of a world only two miles in diameter. That brilliant star sinking swiftly in the west was the light of *Prometheus*, the ship that had brought him here across so many millions of miles of space. She was hanging up there among the stars, wondering why his pod had not returned like a homing pigeon to its roost. In a few minutes she would have passed from sight, dropping below the horizon in her perpetual game of hide-and-seek with the sun.

That was a game that he had lost. He was still on the night side of the asteroid, in the cool safety of its shadow, but the short night would be ending soon. The four-hour day of Icarus was spinning him swiftly towards that dreadful dawn, when a sun thirty times larger than ever shone upon Earth would blast these rocks with fire. Sherrard knew all too well why everything around him was burned and blackened. Icarus was still a week from perihelion but the temperature at noon had already reached a thousand degrees Fahrenheit.

Though this was no time for humour, he suddenly remembered Captain McClellan's description of Icarus: 'The hottest piece of real estate in the solar system.' The truth of that jest had been proved, only a few days before, by one of those simple and unscientific experiments that are so much more impressive than any number of graphs and instrument readings.

Just before daybreak, someone had propped a piece of wood on the summit of one of the tiny hills. Sherrard had been watching, from the safety of the night side, when the first rays of the rising sun had touched the hilltop. When his eyes had adjusted to the sudden detonation of light, he saw that the wood was already beginning to blacken and char. Had there been an atmosphere here, the stick would have burst into flames; such was dawn, upon Icarus . . .

Yet it had not been impossibly hot at the time of their first landing, when they were passing the orbit of Venus five weeks ago. *Prometheus* had overtaken the asteroid as it was beginning its plunge towards the sun, had matched speed with the little world and had touched down upon its surface as lightly as a snowflake. (A snowflake on Icarus – *that* was quite a thought . . .) Then the scientists had fanned out across the fifteen square miles of jagged nickel-iron that covered most of the asteroid's surface, setting up their instruments and checkpoints, collecting samples and making endless observations.

Everything had been carefully planned, years in advance, as part of the International Astrophysical Decade. Here was a unique opportunity for a research ship to get within a mere seventeen million miles of the sun, protected from its fury by a two-mile thick shield of rock and iron. In the shadow of Icarus, the ship could ride safely round the central fire which warmed all the planets, and upon which the existence of all life depended. As the Prometheus of legend had brought the gift of fire to mankind, so the ship that bore his name would return to Earth with other unimagined secrets from the heavens.

There had been plenty of time to set up the instruments and make the surveys before *Prometheus* had to take off and seek the permanent shade of night. Even then, it was still possible for men in the tiny self-propelled space-pods – miniature spaceships, only ten feet long – to work on the night side for an hour or so, as long as they were not overtaken by the advancing line of sunrise. That had seemed a simple-enough condition to meet, on a world where dawn marched forward at only a mile an hour; but Sherrard had failed to meet it, and the penalty was death.

He was still not quite sure what had happened. He had been replacing a seismograph transmitter at Station 145, unofficially known as Mount Everest because it was a full ninety feet above the surrounding territory. The job had been a perfectly straightforward one, even though he had to do it by remote control through the mechanical arms of his pod. Sherrard was an expert at manipulating these; he could tie knots with his metal fingers almost as quickly as with his flesh-and-bone ones. The task had taken little more than twenty minutes, and then the radioseismograph was on the air again, monitoring the tiny quakes and shudders that racked Icarus in ever-increasing numbers as the asteroid approached the sun. It was small satisfaction to know that he had now made a king-sized addition to the record.

After he had checked the signals, he had carefully replaced the sun screens around the instrument. It was hard to believe that two flimsy sheets of polished metal foil, no thicker than paper, could turn aside a flood of radiation that would melt lead or tin within seconds. But the first screen reflected more than ninety per cent of the sunlight falling upon its mirror surface and the second turned back most of the rest, so that only a harmless fraction of the heat passed through.

He had reported completion of the job, received an acknowledgment from the ship, and prepared to head for home. The brilliant floodlights hanging from *Prometheus* – without which the night side of the asteroid would have been in utter darkness – had been an unmistakable target in the sky. The ship was only two miles up, and in this feeble gravity he could have jumped that distance had he been wearing a planetary-type space-suit with flexible legs. As it was, the low-powered micro-rockets of his pod would get him there in a leisurely five minutes.

He had aimed the pod with its gyros, set the rear jets at Strength Two, and pressed the firing button. There had been a violent explosion somewhere in the vicinity of his feet and he had soared away from Icarus – but not towards the ship. Something was horribly wrong; he was tossed to one side of the vehicle, unable to reach the controls. Only one of the jets was firing, and he was pinwheeling across the sky, spinning faster and faster under the off-balanced drive. He tried to find the cut-off, but the spin had completely disorientated him. When he was able to locate the controls, his first reaction made matters worse – he pushed the throttle over to full, like a nervous driver stepping on the accelerator instead of the brake. It took only a second to correct the mistake and kill the jet, but by then he was spinning so rapidly that the stars were wheeling round in circles.

Everything had happened so quickly that there was no time for fear, no time even to call the ship and report what was happening. He took his hands away from the controls; to touch them now would only make matters worse. It would take two or three minutes of cautious jockeying to unravel his spin, and from the flickering glimpses of the approaching rocks it was obvious that he did not have as many seconds. Sherrard remembered a piece of advice at the front of the *Spaceman's Manual*: 'When you don't know what to do, *do nothing*.' He was still doing it when Icarus fell upon him, and the stars went out.

It had been a miracle that the pod was unbroken, and that he was not breathing space. (Thirty minutes from now he might be glad to do so, when the capsule's heat insulation began to fail ...) There had been some damage, of course. The rear-view mirrors, just outside the dome of transparent plastic that enclosed his head, were both snapped off, so that he could no longer see what lay behind him without twisting his neck. This was a trivial mishap; far more serious was the fact that his radio antennas had been torn away by the impact. He could not call the ship, and the ship could not call him. All that came over the radio was a faint crackling, probably produced inside the set itself. He was absolutely alone, cut off from the rest of the human race.

It was a desperate situation, but there was one faint ray of hope. He was not, after all, completely helpless. Even if he could not use the pod's rockets – he guessed that the starboard motor had blown back and ruptured a fuel line, something the designers said was impossible – he was still able to move. He had his arms.

But which way should he crawl? He had lost all sense of location, for though he had taken off from Mount Everest, he might now be thousands of feet away from it. There were no recognizable landmarks in his tiny world; the rapidly sinking star of *Prometheus* was his best guide, and if he could keep the ship in view he would be safe. It would only be a matter of minutes before his absence was noted, if indeed it had not been discovered already. Yet without radio, it might take his colleagues a long time to find him; small though Icarus was, its fifteen square miles of fantastically rugged no man's land could provide an effective hiding place for a ten-foot cylinder. It might take an hour to locate him – which meant that he would have to keep ahead of the murderous sunrise.

He slipped his fingers into the controls that worked his mechanical limbs. Outside the pod, in the hostile vacuum that surrounded him, his substitute arms came to life. They reached down, thrust against the iron surface of the asteroid, and levered the pod from the ground. Sherrard flexed them, and the capsule jerked forward, like some weird, two-legged insect ... first the right arm, then the left, then the right ...

It was less difficult than he had feared, and for the first time he felt his confidence return. Though his mechanical arms had been designed for light precision work, it needed very little pull to set the capsule moving in this weightless environment. The gravity of Icarus was ten thousand times weaker than Earth's: Sherrard and his space-pod weighed less than an ounce here, and once he had set himself in motion he floated forward with an effortless, dreamlike ease.

Yet that very effortlessness had its dangers. He had travelled several hundred yards, and was rapidly overhauling the sinking star of the *Prometheus*, when overconfidence betrayed him. (Strange how quickly the mind could switch from one extreme to the other; a few minutes ago he had been steeling himself to face death – now he was wondering if he would be late for dinner.) Perhaps the novelty of the movement, so unlike anything he had ever attempted before, was responsible for the catastrophe; or perhaps he was still suffering from the after-effects of the crash.

Like all astronauts, Sherrard had learned to orientate himself in space, and had grown accustomed to living and working when the Earthly conceptions of up and down were meaningless. On a world such as Icarus, it was necessary to pretend that there was a real, honest-to-goodness planet 'beneath' your feet, and that when you moved you were travelling over a horizontal plain. If this innocent self-deception failed, you were heading for space vertigo.

The attack came without warning, as it usually did. Quite suddenly, Icarus no longer seemed to be beneath him, the stars no longer above. The universe tilted through a right angle; he was moving straight *up* a vertical cliff, like a mountaineer scaling a rock face, and though Sherrard's reasons told him that this was pure illusion, all his senses screamed that it was true. In a moment gravity must drag him off this sheer wall, and he would drop down mile upon endless mile until he smashed into oblivion.

Worse was to come; the false vertical was still swinging like a compass needle that had lost the pole. Now he was on the *underside* of an immense rocky roof, like a fly clinging to a ceiling; in another moment it would have become a wall again – but this time he would be moving straight down it, instead of up . . .

He had lost all control over the pod, and the clammy sweat that had begun to dew his brow warned him that he would soon lose control over his body. There was only one thing to do; he clenched his eyes tightly shut, squeezed as far back as possible into the tiny closed world of the capsule, and pretended with all his might that the universe outside did not exist. He did not even allow the slow, gentle crunch of his second crash to interfere with his self-hypnosis.

When he again dared to look outside, he found that the pod had come to rest against a large boulder. Its mechanical arms had broken the force of the impact, but at a cost that was more than he could afford to pay. Though the capsule was virtually weightless here, it still possessed its normal five hundred pounds of inertia, and it had been moving at perhaps four miles an hour. The momentum had been too much for the metal arms to absorb; one had snapped, and the other was hopelessly bent.

When he saw what had happened, Sherrard's first reaction was not despair, but anger. He had been so certain of success when the pod had started its glide across the barren face of Icarus. And now this, all through a moment of physical weakness! But space made no allowance for human frailties or emotions, and a man who did not accept that fact had no right to be here.

At least he had gained precious time in his pursuit of the ship; he had put an extra ten minutes, if not more, between himself and dawn. Whether that ten minutes would merely prolong the agony or whether it would give his shipmates the extra time they needed to find him, he would soon know.

Where were they? Surely they had started the search by now! He strained his eyes towards the brilliant star of the ship, hoping to pick out the fainter lights of space-pods moving towards him – but nothing else was visible against the slowly turning vault of heaven.

He had better look to his own resources, slender though they were. Only a few minutes were left before the *Prometheus* and her trailing lights would sink below the edge of the asteroid and leave him in darkness. It was true that the darkness would be all to brief, but before it fell upon him he might find some shelter against the coming day. This rock into which he had crashed, for example ...

Yes, it would give some shade, until the sun was half-way up the sky. Nothing could protect him if it passed right overhead; but it was just possible that he might be in a latitude where the sun never rose far above the horizon at this season of Icarus' four-hundred-and-nine-day year. Then he might survive the brief period of daylight; that was his only hope, if the rescuers did not find him before dawn.

There went *Prometheus* and her lights, below the edge of the world. With her going, the now-unchallenged stars blazed forth with redoubled brilliance. More glorious than any of them – so lovely that even to look upon it almost brought tears to his eyes – was the blazing beacon of Earth, with its companion moon beside it. He had been born on one, and had walked on the other; would he see either again?

Strange that until now he had given no thought to his wife and children, and to all that he loved in the life that now seemed so far away. He felt a spasm of guilt, but it passed swiftly. The ties of affection were not weakened, even across the hundred million miles of space that now sundered him from his family. At this moment, they were simply irrelevant. He was now a primitive, self-centred animal fighting for his life, and his only weapon was his brain. In this conflict, there was no place for the heart; it would merely be a hindrance, spoiling his judgment and weakening his resolution.

And then he saw something that banished all thoughts of his distant home. Reaching up above the horizon behind him, spreading across the stars like a milky mist, was a faint and ghostly cone of phosphorescence. It was the herald of the sun – the beautiful, pearly phantom of the corona, visible on Earth only during the rare moments of a total eclipse. When the corona was rising, the sun would not be far behind, to smite this little land with fury.

Sherrard made good use of the warning. Now he could judge, with some accuracy, the exact point where the sun would rise. Crawling slowly and clumsily on the broken stumps of his metal arms, he dragged the capsule round to the side of the boulder that should give the greatest shade. He had barely reached it when the sun was upon him like a beast of prey, and his tiny world exploded into light.

He raised the dark filters inside his helmet, one thickness

after another, until he could endure the glare. Except where the broad shadow of the boulder lay across the asteroid, it was like looking into a furnace. Every detail of the desolate land around him was revealed by that merciless light; there were no greys, only blinding whites and impenetrable blacks. All the shadowed cracks and hollows were pools of ink, while the higher ground already seemed to be on fire, as it caught the sun. Yet it was only a minute after dawn.

Now Sherrard could understand how the scorching heat of a billion summers had turned Icarus into a cosmic cinder, baking the rocks until the last traces of gas had bubbled out of them. Why should men travel, he asked himself bitterly, across the gulf of stars at such expense and risk – merely to land on a spinning slag heap? For the same reason, he knew, that they once struggled to reach Everest and the Poles and the far places of the Earth – for the excitement of the body that was adventure, and the more enduring excitement of the mind that was discovery. It was an answer that gave him little consolation, now that he was about to be grilled like a joint on the turning spit of Icarus.

Already he could feel the first breath of heat upon his face. The boulder against which he was lying gave him protection from direct sunlight, but the glare reflected back at him from those blazing rocks only a few yards away was striking through the transparent plastic of the dome. It would grow swiftly more intense as the sun rose higher; he had even less time than he had thought, and with the knowledge came a kind of numb resignation that was beyond fear. He would wait – if he could – until the sunrise engulfed him and the capsule's cooling unit gave up the unequal struggle; then he would crack the pod and let the air gush out into the vacuum of space.

Nothing to do but to sit and think in the minutes that were left to him before his pool of shadow contracted. He did not try to direct his thoughts, but let them wander where they willed. How strange that he should be dying now, because back in the nineteen-forties – years before he was born – a man at Palomar had spotted a streak of light on a photographic plate, and had named it so appropriately after the boy who flew too near the sun.

One day, he supposed, they would build a monument here for him on this blistered plain. What would they inscribe upon it? 'Here died Colin Sherrard, astronics engineer, in the cause of Science.' That would be funny, for he had never understood half the things that the scientists were trying to do.

Yet some of the excitement of their discoveries had communicated itself to him. He remembered how the geologists had scraped away the charred skin of the asteroid, and had polished the metallic surface that lay beneath. It had been covered with a curious pattern of lines and scratches, like one of the abstract paintings of the Post-Picasso Decadents. But these lines had some meaning; they wrote the history of Icarus, though only a geologist could read it. They revealed, so Sherrard had been told, that this lump of iron and rock had not always floated alone in space. At some remote time in the past, it had been under enormous pressure – and that could mean only one thing. Billions of years ago it had been part of a much larger body, perhaps, a planet like Earth. For some reason that planet had blown up, and Icarus and all the thousands of other asteroids were the fragments of that cosmic explosion.

Even at this moment, as the incandescent line of sunlight came closer, this was a thought that stirred his mind. What Sherrard was lying upon was the core of a world – perhaps a world that had once known life. In a strange, irrational way it comforted him to know that his might not be the only ghost to haunt Icarus until the end of time.

The helmet was misting up; that could only mean that the cooling unit was about to fail. It had done its work well;

69

even now, though the rocks only a few yards away must be glowing a sullen red, the heat inside the capsule was not unendurable. When failure came, it would be sudden and catastrophic.

He reached for the red lever that would rob the sun of its prey – but before he pulled it, he would look for the last time upon Earth. Cautiously, he lowered the dark filters, adjusting them so that they still cut out the glare from the rocks, but no longer blocked his view of space.

The stars were faint now, dimmed by the advancing glow of the corona. And just visible over the boulder whose shield would soon fail him was a stub of crimson flame, a crooked finger of fire jutting from the edge of the sun itself. He had only seconds left.

There was the Earth, there was the moon. Good-bye to them both, and to his friends and loved ones on each of them. While he was looking at the sky, the sunlight had begun to lick the base of the capsule, and he felt the first touch of fire. In a reflex as automatic as it was useless, he drew up his legs, trying to escape the advancing wave of heat.

What was that? A brilliant flash of light, infinitely brighter than any of the stars, had suddenly exploded overhead. Miles above him, a huge mirror was sailing across the sky, reflecting the sunlight as it slowly turned through space. Such a thing was utterly impossible; he was beginning to suffer from hallucinations, and it was time he took his leave. Already the sweat was pouring from his body, and in a few seconds the capsule would be a furnace.

He waited no longer, but pulled on the Emergency Release with all his waning strength, bracing himself at the same moment to face the end.

Nothing happened; the lever would not move. He tugged it again and again before he realized that it was hopelessly jammed. There was no easy way out for him, no merciful

70

death as the air gushed from his lungs. It was then, as the true terror of his situation struck home to him, that his nerve finally broke and he began to scream like a trapped animal.

When he heard Captain McClellan's voice speaking to him, thin but clear, he knew that it must be another hallucination. Yet some last remnant of discipline and self-control checked his screaming; he clenched his teeth and listened to that familiar, commanding voice.

'Sherrard! Hold on, man! We've got a fix on you – but keep shouting!'

'Here I am!' he cried, 'but hurry, for God's sake! I'm burning!'

Deep down in what was left of his rational mind he realized what had happened. Some feeble ghost of a signal was leaking through the broken stubs of his antennas, and the searchers had heard his screams – as he was hearing their voices. That meant they must be very close indeed, and the knowledge gave him sudden strength.

He stared through the steaming plastic of the dome, looking once more for that impossible mirror in the sky. There it was again – and now he realized that the baffling perspectives of space had tricked his senses. The mirror was not miles away, nor was it huge. It was almost on top of him, and it was moving fast.

He was still shouting when it slid across the face of the rising sun, and its blessed shadow fell upon him like a cool wind that had blown out of the heart of winter, over leagues of snow and ice. Now that it was so close, he recognized it at once; it was merely a large metal-foil radiation screen, no doubt hastily snatched from one of the instrument sites. In the safety of its shadow, his friends had been searching for him.

A heavy-duty, two-man capsule was hovering overhead, holding the glittering shield in one set of arms and reaching for him with the other. Even through the misty dome and the haze of heat that still sapped his senses, he recognized Captain McClellan's anxious face, looking down at him from the other pod.

So this was what birth was like, for truly he had been reborn. He was too exhausted for gratitude – that would come later – but as he rose from the burning rocks his eyes sought and found the bright star of Earth. 'Here I am,' he said silently. 'I'm coming back.'

Back to enjoy and cherish all the beauties of the world he had thought were lost forever. No – not all of them.

He would never enjoy summer again.

DEATH AND THE SENATOR

WASHINGTON had never looked lovelier in the spring; and this was the last spring, thought Senator Steelman bleakly, that he would ever see. Even now, despite all that Dr. Jordan had told him, he could not fully accept the truth. In the past there had always been a way of escape; no defeat had been final. When men had betrayed him, he had discarded them – even ruined them, as a warning to others. But now the betrayal was within himself; already, it seemed, he could feel the laboured beating of the heart that would soon be stilled. No point in planning now for the Presidential election of 1976; he might not even live to see the nominations ...

It was an end of dreams and ambition, and he could not console himself with the knowledge that for all men these must end someday. For him it was too soon; he thought of Cecil Rhodes, who had always been one of his heroes, crying 'So much to do – so little time to do it in!' as he died before his fiftieth birthday. He was already older than Rhodes, and had done far less.

The car was taking him away from the Capitol; there was symbolism in that, and he tried not to dwell upon it. Now he was abreast of the New Smithsonian – that vast complex of museums he had never had time to visit, though he had watched it spread along the Mall throughout the years he had been in Washington. How much he had missed, he told himself bitterly, in his relentless pursuit of power. The whole universe of art and culture had remained almost closed to him, and that was only part of the price that he had paid. He had become a stranger to his family and to

73

those who were once his friends. Love had been sacrificed on the altar of ambition, and the sacrifice had been in vain. Was there anyone in all the world who would weep at his departure?

Yes, there was. The feeling of utter desolation relaxed its grip upon his soul. As he reached for the phone, he felt ashamed that he had to call the office to get this number, when his mind was cluttered with memories of so many less important things.

(There was the White House, almost dazzling in the spring sunshine. For the first time in his life he did not give it a second glance. Already it belonged to another world – a world that would never concern him again.)

The car circuit had no vision, but he did not need it to sense Irene's mild surprise – and her still milder pleasure.

'Hello, Renee – how are you all?'

'Fine, Dad. When are we going to see you?'

It was the polite formula his daughter always used on the rare occasions when he called. And invariably, except at Christmas or birthdays, his answer was a vague promise to drop around at some indefinite future date.

'I was wondering,' he said slowly, almost apologetically, 'if I could borrow the children for an afternoon. It's a long time since I've taken them out, and I felt like getting away from the office.'

'But of course,' Irene answered, her voice warming with pleasure. 'They'll love it. When would you like them?'

'Tomorrow would be fine. I could call around twelve, and take them to the Zoo or the Smithsonian, or anywhere else they felt like visiting.'

Now she was really startled, for she knew well enough that he was one of the busiest men in Washington, with a schedule planned weeks in advance. She would be wondering what had happened; he hoped she would not guess the truth. No reason why she should, for not even his secretary

74

knew of the stabbing pains that had driven him to seek this long-overdue medical checkup.

'That would be wonderful. They were talking about you only yesterday, asking when they'd see you again.'

His eyes misted, and he was glad that Renee could not see him.

'I'll be there at noon,' he said hastily, trying to keep the emotion out of his voice. 'My love to you all.' He switched off before she could answer, and relaxed against the upholstery with a sigh of relief. Almost upon impulse, without conscious planning, he had taken the first step in the reshaping of his life. Though his own children were lost to him, a bridge across the generations remained intact. If he did nothing else, he must guard and strengthen it in the months that were left.

Taking two lively and inquisitive children through the natural-history building was not what the doctor would have ordered, but it was what he wanted to do. Joey and Susan had grown so much since their last meeting, and it required both physical and mental alertness to keep up with them. No sooner had they entered the rotunda than they broke away from him, and scampered towards the enormous elephant dominating the marble hall.

'What's that?' cried Joey.

'It's an elephant, stupid,' answered Susan with all the crushing superiority of her seven years.

'I know it's an effelant,' retorted Joey. 'But what's its name?'

Senator Steelman scanned the label, but found no assistance there. This was one occasion when the risky adage 'Sometimes wrong, never uncertain' was a safe guide to conduct.

'He was called – er – Jumbo,' he said hastily. 'Just look at those tusks!'

'Did he ever get toothache?'

'Oh no.'

'Then how did he clean his teeth? Ma says that if I don't clean mine ...'

Steelman saw where the logic of this was leading, and thought it best to change the subject.

'There's a lot more to see inside. Where do you want to start – birds, snakes, fish, mammals?'

'Snakes!' clamoured Susan. 'I wanted to keep one in a box, but Daddy said no. Do you think he'd change his mind if you asked him?'

'What's a mammal?' asked Joey, before Steelman could work out an answer to that.

'Come along,' he said firmly. 'I'll show you.'

As they moved through the halls and galleries, the children darting from one exhibit to another, he felt at peace with the world. There was nothing like a museum for calming the mind, for putting the problems of everyday life in their true perspective. Here, surrounded by the infinite variety and wonder of Nature, he was reminded of truths he had forgotten. He was only one of a million million creatures that shared this planet Earth. The entire human race, with its hopes and fears, its triumphs and its follies, might be no more than an incident in the history of the world. As he stood before the monstrous bones of Diplodocus (the children for once awed and silent), he felt the winds of Eternity blowing through his soul. He could no longer take so seriously the gnawing of ambition, the belief that he was the man the nation needed. *What* nation, if it came to that? A mere two centuries ago this summer, the Declaration of Independence had been signed; but this old American had lain in the Utah rocks for a hundred million years ...

He was tired when they reached the Hall of Oceanic Life, with its dramatic reminder that Earth still possessed animals greater than any that the past could show. The ninety-foot blue whale plunging into the ocean, and all the other swift hunters of the sea, brought back memories of hours he had once spent on a tiny, glistening deck with a white sail billowing above him. That was another time when he had known contentment, listening to the swish of water past the prow, and the sighing of the wind through the rigging. He had not sailed for thirty years; this was another of the world's pleasures he had put aside.

'I don't like fish,' complained Susan. 'When do we get to the snakes?'

'Presently,' he said. 'But what's the hurry? There's plenty of time.'

The words slipped out before he realized it. He checked his step, while the children ran on ahead. Then he smiled, without bitterness. For in a sense, it was true enough. There *was* plenty of time. Each day, each hour could be a universe of experience, if one used it properly. In the last weeks of his life, he would begin to live.

As yet, no one at the office suspected anything. Even his outing with the children had not caused much surprise; he had done such things before, suddenly cancelling his appointments and leaving his staff to pick up the pieces. The pattern of his behaviour had not yet changed, but in a few days it would be obvious to all his associates that something had happened. He owed it to them – and to the party – to break the news as soon as possible; there were, however, many personal decisions he had to make first, which he wished to settle in his own mind before he began the vast unwinding of his affairs.

There was another reason for his hesitancy. During his career, he had seldom lost a fight, and in the cut and thrust of political life he had given quarter to none. Now, facing his ultimate defeat, he dreaded the sympathy and the condolences that his many enemies would hasten to shower upon him. The attitude, he knew, was a foolish one – a remnant of his stubborn pride which was too much a part of his personality to vanish even under the shadow of death.

He carried his secret from committee room to White House to Capitol, and through all the labyrinths of Washington society, for more than two weeks. It was the finest performance of his career, but there was no one to appreciate it. At the end of that time he had completed his plan of action; it remained only to dispatch a few letters he had written in his own hand, and to call his wife.

The office located her, not without difficulty, in Rome. She was still beautiful, he thought, as her features swam on to the screen; she would have made a fine First Lady, and that would have been some compensation for the lost years. As far as he knew, she had looked forward to the prospect; but had he ever really understood what she wanted?

'Hello, Martin,' she said, 'I was expecting to hear from you, I suppose you want me to come back.'

'Are you willing to?' he asked quietly. The gentleness of his voice obviously surprised her.

'I'd be a fool to say no, wouldn't I? But if they don't elect you, I want to go my own way again. You must agree to that.'

'They won't elect me. They won't even nominate me. You're the first to know this, Diana. In six months, I shall be dead.'

The directness was brutal, but it had a purpose. That fraction-of-a-second delay with the radio waves flashed up to the communication satellites and back again to Earth had never seemed so long. For once, he had broken through the beautiful mask. Her eyes widened with disbelief, her hand flew to her lips.

'You're joking!'

'About *this*? It's true enough. My heart's worn out. Dr. Jordan told me, a couple of weeks ago. It's my own fault, of course, but let's not go into that.'

'So that's why you've been taking out the children: I wondered what had happened.'

He might have guessed that Irene would have talked with her mother. It was a sad reflection on Martin Steelman, if so commonplace a fact as showing an interest in his own grandchildren could cause curiosity.

'Yes,' he admitted frankly. 'I'm afraid I left it a little late. Now I'm trying to make up for lost time. Nothing else seems very important.'

In silence, they looked into each other's eyes across the curve of the Earth, and across the empty desert of the dividing years. Then Diana answered, a little unsteadily, 'I'll start packing right away.'

Now that the news was out, he felt a great sense of relief. Even the sympathy of his enemies was not as hard to accept as he had feared. For overnight, indeed, he had no enemies. Men who had not spoken to him in years, except with invective, sent messages whose sincerity could not be doubted. Ancient quarrels evaporated, or turned out to be founded on misunderstandings. It was a pity that one had to die to learn these things ...

He also learned that, for a man of affairs, dying was a full-time job. There were successors to appoint, legal and financial mazes to untangle, committee and state business to wind up. The work of an energetic lifetime could not be terminated suddenly, as one switches off an electric light. It was astonishing how many responsibilities he had acquired, and how difficult it was to divest himself of them. He had never found it easy to delegate power (a fatal flaw, many critics had said, in a man who hoped to be Chief Executive), but now he must do so, before it slipped forever from his hands.

It was as if a great clock was running down, and there was

no one to rewind it. As he gave away his books, read and destroyed old letters, closed useless accounts and files, dictated final instructions, and wrote farewell notes, he sometimes felt a sense of complete unreality. There was no pain; he could never have guessed that he did not have years of active life ahead of him. Only a few lines on a cardiogram lay like a roadblock across his future – or like a curse, written in some strange language the doctors alone could read.

Almost every day now Diana, Irene, or her husband brought the children to see him. In the past he had never felt at ease with Bill, but that, he knew, had been his own fault. You could not expect a son-in-law to replace a son, and it was unfair to blame Bill because he had not been cast in the image of Martin Steelman, Jr. Bill was a person in his own right; he had looked after Irene, made her happy, and fathered her children. That he lacked ambition was a flaw – if flaw indeed it was – that the Senator could at last forgive.

He could even think, without pain or bitterness, of his own son, who had travelled this road before him and now lay, one cross among many, in the United Nations cemetery at Capetown. He had never visited Martin's grave; in the days when he had the time, white men were not popular in what was left of South Africa. Now he could go if he wished, but he was uncertain if it would be fair to harrow Diana with such a mission. His own memories would not trouble him much longer, but she would be left with hers.

Yet he would like to go, and felt it was his duty. Moreover, it would be a last treat for the children. To them it would be only a holiday in a strange land, without any tinge of sorrow for an uncle they had never known. He had started to make the arrangements when, for the second time within a month his whole world was turned upside down.

Even now, a dozen or more visitors would be waiting for him each morning when he arrived at his office. Not as many as in the old days, but still a sizable crowd. He had never imagined, however, that Dr. Harkness would be among them.

The sight of that thin, gangling figure made him momentarily break his stride. He felt his cheeks flush, his pulse quicken at the memory of ancient battles across committee-room tables, of angry exchanges that had reverberated along the myriad channels of the ether. Then he relaxed; as far as he was concerned, all that was over.

Harkness rose to his feet, a little awkwardly, as he approached. Senator Steelman knew that initial embarrassment – he had seen it so often in the last few weeks. Everyone he now met was automatically at a disadvantage, always on the alert to avoid the one subject that was taboo.

'Well, Doctor,' he said. 'This is a surprise – I never expected to see *you* here.'

He could not resist that little jab, and derived some satisfaction at watching it go home. But it was free from bitterness, as the other's smile acknowledged.

'Senator,' replied Harkness, in a voice that was pitched so low that he had to lean forward to hear it, 'I've some extremely important information for you. Can we speak alone for a few minutes? It won't take long.'

Steelman nodded; he had his own ideas of what was important now, and felt only a mild curiosity as to why the scientist had come to see him. The man seemed to have changed a good deal since their last encounter, seven years ago. He was much more assured and self-confident, and had lost the nervous mannerisms that had helped to make him such an unconvincing witness.

'Senator,' he began, when they were alone in the private office, 'I've some news that may be quite a shock to you. I believe that you can be cured.'

Steelman slumped heavily in his chair. This was the one thing he had never expected; from the first, he had not encumbered himself with the burden of vain hopes. Only a fool fought against the inevitable, and he had accepted his fate.

For a moment he could not speak; then he looked up at his old adversary and gasped: 'Who told you that? All my doctors —'

'Never mind them; it's not their fault they're ten years behind the times. Look at this.'

'What does it mean? I can't read Russian.'

'It's the latest issue of the USSR *Journal of Space Medicine*. It arrived a few days ago, and we did the usual routine translation. This note here – the one I've marked – refers to some recent work at the Mechnikov Station.'

'What's that?'

'You don't *know*? Why, that's their Satellite Hospital, the one they've built just below the Great Radiation Belt.'

'Go on,' said Steelman, in a voice that was suddenly dry and constricted. 'I'd forgotten they'd called it that.' He had hoped to end his life in peace, but now the past had come back to haunt him.

'Well, the note itself doesn't say much, but you can read a lot between the lines. It's one of those advance hints that scientists put out before they have time to write a full-fledged paper, so they can claim priority later. The title is: "Therapeutic Effects of Zero Gravity on Circulatory Diseases." What they've done is to induce heart disease artificially in rabbits and hamsters, and then take them up to the space station. In orbit, of course, nothing has any weight; the heart and muscles have practically no work to do. And the result is exactly what I tried to tell you, years ago. Even extreme cases can be arrested, and many can be cured.'

The tiny, panelled office that had been the centre of his world, the scene of so many conferences, the birthplace of

82

so many plans, became suddenly unreal. Memory was much more vivid: he was back again at those hearings, in the fall of 1969, when the National Aeronautics and Space Administration's first decade of activity had been under review – and, frequently, under fire.

He had never been chairman of the Senate Committee on Astronautics, but he had been its most vocal and effective member. It was here that he had made his reputation as a guardian of the public purse, as a hardheaded man who could not be bamboozled by utopian scientific dreamers. He had done a good job; from that moment, he had never been far from the headlines. It was not that he had any particular feeling for space and science, but he knew a live issue when he saw one. Like a tape-recorder unrolling in his mind, it all came back ...

'Dr. Harkness, you are Technical Director of the National Aeronautics and Space Administration?'

'That is correct.'

'I have here the figures for NASA's expenditure over the period 1959–69; they are quite impressive. At the moment the total is $82,547,450,000, and the estimate for fiscal 69–70 is well over ten billions. Perhaps you could give us some indication of the return we can expect from all this.'

'I'll be glad to do so, Senator.'

That was how it had started, on a firm but not unfriendly note. The hostility had crept in later. That it was unjustified, he had known at the time; any big organization had weaknesses and failures, and one which literally aimed at the stars could never hope for more than partial success. From the beginning, it had been realized that the conquest of space would be at least as costly in lives and treasure as the conquest of the air. In ten years, almost a hundred men had died – on Earth, in space, and upon the barren surface of the Moon. Now that the urgency of the early sixties was over, the public was asking 'Why?' Steelman was shrewd enough to see himself as mouthpiece for those questioning voices. His performance had been cold and calculated; it was convenient to have a scapegoat, and Dr. Harkness was unlucky enough to be cast for the role.

'Yes, Doctor, I understand all the benefits we've received from space research in the way of improved communications and weather forecasting, and I'm sure everyone appreciates them. But almost all this work has been done with automatic, unmanned vehicles. What I'm worried about – what many people are worried about – is the mounting expense of the Man-in-Space programme, and its very marginal utility. Since the original Dyna-Soar and Apollo projects almost a decade ago, we've shot billions of dollars into space. And with what result? So that a mere handful of men can spend a few uncomfortable hours outside the atmosphere; achieving nothing that television cameras and automatic equipment couldn't do – much better and cheaper. And the lives that have been lost! None of us will forget those screams we heard coming over the radio when the X-21 burned up on re-entry. What right have we to send men to such deaths?'

He could still remember the hushed silence in the committee chamber when he had finished. His questions were very reasonable ones, and deserved to be answered. What was unfair was the rhetorical manner in which he had framed them and, above all, the fact that they were aimed at a man who could not answer them effectively. Steelman would not have tried such tactics on a von Braun or a Rickover; they would have given him at least as good as they received. But Harkness was no orator; if he had deep personal feelings, he kept them to himself. He was a good scientist, an able administrator – and a poor witness. It had been like shooting fish in a barrel. The reporters had loved it; he never knew which of them coined the nickname

'Hapless Harkness'.

'Now this plan of yours, Doctor, for a fifty-man space laboratory – *how* much did you say it would cost?'

'I've already told you – just under one and a half billions.'

'And the annual maintenance?'

Not more than $250,000,000.'

'When we consider what's happened to previous estimates, you will forgive us if we look upon these figures with some scepticism. But even assuming that they are right, what will we get for the money?'

'We will be able to establish our first large-scale research station in space. So far, we have had to do our experimenting in cramped quarters aboard unsuitable vehicles, usually when they were engaged on some other mission. A permanent, manned satellite laboratory is essential. Without it, further progress is out of the question. Astrobiology can hardly get started —'

'Astro what?'

'Astrobiology – the study of living organisms in space. The Russians really started it when they sent up the dog Laika in Sputnik II and they're still ahead of us in this field. But no one's done any serious work on insects or invertebrates – in fact, on any animals except dogs, mice, and monkeys.'

'I see. Would I be correct in saying that you would like funds for building a zoo in space?'

The laughter in the committee room had helped to kill the project. And it had helped, Senator Steelman now realized, to kill him.

He had only himself to blame, for Dr. Harkness had tried, in his ineffectual way, to outline the benefits that a space laboratory might bring. He had particularly stressed the medical aspects, promising nothing but pointing out the possibilities. Surgeons, he had suggested, would be able to develop new techniques in an environment where the organs had no weight; men might live longer, freed from the wear and tear of gravity, for the strain on heart and muscles would be enormously reduced. Yes, he had mentioned the heart; but that had been of no interest to Senator Steelman – healthy, and ambitious, and anxious to make good copy ...

'Why have you come to tell me this?' he said dully. 'Couldn't you let me die in peace?'

'That's the point,' said Harkness impatiently. 'There's no need to give up hope.'

'Because the Russians have cured some hamsters and rabbits?'

'They've done much more than that. The paper I showed you only quoted the preliminary results; it's already a year out of date. They don't want to raise false hopes, so they are keeping as quiet as possible.'

'How do you know this?'

Harkness looked surprised.

'Why, I called Professor Stanyukovitch, my opposite number. It turned out that he was up on the Mechnikov Station, which proves how important they consider this work. He's an old friend of mine, and I took the liberty of mentioning your case.'

The dawn of hope, after its long absence, can be as painful as its departure. Steelman found it hard to breathe and for a dreadful moment he wondered if the final attack had come. But it was only excitement; the constriction in his chest relaxed, the ringing in his ears faded away, and he heard Dr. Harkness' voice saying: 'He wanted to know if you could come to Astrograd right away, so I said I'd ask you. If you can make it, there's a flight from New York at ten-thirty tomorrow morning.'

Tomorrow he had promised to take the children to the Zoo; it would be the first time he had let them down. The thought gave him a sharp stab of guilt, and it required almost an effort of will to answer: 'I can make it.'

He saw nothing of Moscow during the few minutes that the big intercontinental ramjet fell down from the stratosphere. The view-screens were switched off during the descent, for the sight of the ground coming straight up as a ship fell vertically on its sustaining jets was highly disconcerting to passengers.

At Moscow he changed to a comfortable but old-fashioned turboprop, and as he flew eastward into the night he had his first real opportunity for reflection. It was a very strange question to ask himself, but was he altogether glad that the future was no longer wholly certain? His life, which a few hours ago had seemed so simple, had suddenly become complex again, as it opened out once more into possibilities he had learned to put aside. Dr. Johnson had been right when he said that nothing settles a man's mind more wonderfully than the knowledge that he will be hanged in the morning. For the converse was certainly true – nothing unsettled it so much as the thought of a reprieve.

He was asleep when they touched down at Astrograd, the space capital of the U.S.S.R. When the gentle impact of the landing shook him awake, for a moment he could not imagine where he was. Had he dreamed that he was flying halfway around the world in search of life? No; it was not a dream, but it might well be a wild-goose chase.

Twelve hours later, he was still waiting for the answer. The last instrument reading had been taken; the spots of light on the cardiograph display had ceased their fateful dance. The familiar routine of the medical examination and the gentle, competent voices of the doctors and nurses had done much to relax his mind. And it was very restful in the softly lit reception room, where the specialists had asked him to wait while they conferred together. Only the Russian magazines, and a few portraits of somewhat hirsute pioneers of Soviet medicine, reminded him that he was no longer in his own country.

He was not the only patient. About a dozen men and women, of all ages, were sitting around the wall, reading magazines and trying to appear at ease. There was no conversation, no attempt to catch anyone's eye. Every soul in this room was in his private limbo, suspended between life and death. Though they were linked together by a common misfortune, the link did not extend to communication. Each seemed as cut off from the rest of the human race as if he was already speeding through the cosmic gulfs where lay his only hope.

But in the far corner of the room, there was an exception. A young couple – neither could have been more than twenty-five – were huddling together in such desperate misery that at first Steelman found the spectacle annoying. No matter how bad their own problems, he told himself severely, people should be more considerate. They should hide their emotions – especially in a place like this, where they might upset others.

His annoyance quickly turned to pity, for no heart can remain untouched for long at the sight of simple, unselfish love in deep distress. As the minutes dripped away in a silence broken only by the rustling of papers and the scraping of chairs, his pity grew almost to an obsession.

What was their story, he wondered? The boy had sensitive, intelligent features; he might have been an artist, a scientist, a musician – there was no way of telling. The girl was pregnant; she had one of those homely peasant faces so common among Russian women. She was far from beautiful, but sorrow and love had given her features a luminous sweetness. Steelman found it hard to take his eyes from her – for somehow, though there was not the slightest physical resemblance, she reminded him of Diana. Thirty years ago, as they had walked from the church together, he had seen that same glow in the eyes of his wife. He had almost forgotten it; was the fault his, or hers, that it had faded so soon?

Without any warning, his chair vibrated beneath him. A swift, sudden tremor had swept through the building, as if a giant hammer had smashed again the ground, many miles away. An earthquake? Steelman wondered; then he remembered where he was, and started counting seconds.

He gave up when he reached sixty; presumably the sound-proofing was so good that the slower, air-borne noise had not reached him, and only the shock wave through the ground recorded the fact that a thousand tons had just leapt into the sky. Another minute passed before he heard, distant but clear, a sound as of a thunderstorm raging below the edge of the world. It was even more miles away than he had dreamed; what the noise must be like at the launching site was beyond imagination.

Yet that thunder would not trouble him, he knew, when he also rose into the sky; the speeding rocket would leave it far behind. Nor would the thrust of acceleration be able to touch his body, as it rested in its bath of warm water — more comfortable even than this deeply padded chair.

The distant rumble was still rolling back from the edge of space when the door of the waiting room opened and the nurse beckoned to him. Though he felt many eyes following him, he did not look back as he walked out to receive his sentence.

The news services tried to get in contact with him all the way back from Moscow, but he refused to accept the calls. 'Say I'm sleeping and musn't be disturbed,' he told the stewardess. He wondered who had tipped them off, and felt annoyed at this invasion of his privacy. Yet privacy was something he had avoided for years, and had learned

89

to appreciate only in the last few weeks. He could not blame the reporters and commentators if they assumed that he had reverted to type.

They were waiting for him when the ramjet touched down at Washington. He knew most of them by name, and some were old friends, genuinely glad to hear the news that had raced ahead of him.

'What does it feel like, Senator' said Macauley, of *The Times*, 'to know you're back to harness? I take it that it's true – the Russians can cure you?'

'They *think* they can,' he answered cautiously. 'This is a new field of medicine, and no one can promise anything.'

'When do you leave for space?'

'Within the week as soon as I've settled some affairs here.'

'And when will you be back – if it works?'

'That's hard to say. Even if everything goes smoothly, I'll be up there at least six months.'

Involuntarily, he glanced at the sky. At dawn or sunset – even during the daytime, if one knew where to look – the Mechnikov Station was a spectacular sight, more brilliant than any of the stars. But there were now so many satellites of which this was true that only an expert could tell one from another.

'Six months,' said a newsman thoughtfully. 'That means you'll be out of the picture for seventy-six.'

'But nicely in it for 1980,' said another.

'*And* 1984' added a third. There was a general laugh; people were already making jokes about 1984, which had once seemed so far in the future, but would soon be a date no different from any other ... it was hoped.

The ears and the microphones were waiting for his reply. As he stood at the foot of the ramp, once more the focus of attention and curiosity, he felt the old excitement stirring in his veins. What a comeback it would be, to return from space a new man! It would give him a glamour that no other candidate could match; there was something Olympian, almost godlike, about the prospect. Already he found himself trying to work it into his election slogans ...

'Give me time to make my plans,' he said. 'It's going to take me a while to get used to this. But I promise you a statement before I leave Earth.'

Before I leave Earth. Now, there was a fine, dramatic phrase. He was still savouring its rhythm with his mind when he saw Diana coming towards him from the airport buildings.

Already she had changed as he himself was changing; in her eyes was a wariness and reserve that had not been there two days ago. It said, as clearly as any words: 'Is it going to happen, all over again?' Though the day was warm, he felt suddenly cold, as if he had caught a chill on those far Siberian plains.

But Joey and Susan were unchanged, as they ran to greet him. He caught them up in his arms, and buried his face in their hair, so that the cameras would not see the tears that had started from his eyes. As they clung to him in the innocent unselfconscious love of childhood, he knew what his choice would have to be.

They alone had known him when he was free from the itch for power; that was the way they must remember him, if they remembered him at all.

'Your conference call, Mr. Steelman,' said his secretary. 'I'm routing it on to your private screen.'

He swivelled round in his chair and faced the grey panel on the wall. As he did so, it split into two vertical sections. On the right half was a view of an office much like his own, and only a few miles away. But on the left —

Professor Stanyukovitch, lightly dressed in shorts and singlet, was floating in mid-air a good foot above his seat.

He grabbed it when he saw that he had company, pulled himself down, and fastened a webbed belt around his waist. Behind him were ranged banks of communications equipment; and behind those, Steelman knew, was space.

Dr. Harkness spoke first from the right-hand screen.

'We were expecting to hear from you, Senator. Professor Stanyukovitch tells me that everything is ready.'

'The next supply ship' said the Russian, 'comes up in two days. It will be taking me back to Earth but I hope to see you before I leave the station.'

His voice was curiously high-pitched, owing to the thin oxyhelium atmosphere he was breathing. Apart from that, there was no sense of distance, no background of interference. Though Stanyukovitch was thousands of miles away, and racing through space at four miles a second, he might have been in the same office. Steelman could even hear the faint whirring of electric motors from the equipment racks behind him.

'Professor,' answered Steelman, 'there are a few things I'd like to ask before I go.'

'Certainly.'

Now he could tell that Stanyukovitch was a long way off. There was an appreciable time lag before his reply arrived; the station must be above the far side of the Earth.

'When I was at Astrograd I noticed many other patients at the clinic. I was wondering – on what basis do you select those for treatment?'

This time the pause was much greater than the delay due to the sluggish speed of radio waves. Then Stanyukovitch answered: 'Why, those with the best chance of responding.'

'But your accommodation must be very limited. You must have many other candidates besides myself.'

'I don't quite see the point —' interrupted Dr. Harkness, a little too anxiously.

Steelman swung his eyes to the right-hand screen. It was

quite difficult to recognize, in the man staring back at him, the witness who had squirmed beneath his needling only a few years ago. The experience had tempered Harkness, had given him his baptism in the art of politics. Steelman had taught him much, and he had applied his hard-won knowledge.

His motives had been obvious from the first. Harkness would have been less than human if he did not relish this sweetest of revenges, this triumphant vindication of his faith. And as Space Administration Director, he was well aware that half his budget battles would be over when all the world knew that a potential President of the United States was in a Russian space hospital ... because his own country did not possess one.

'Dr. Harkness,' said Steelman gently, 'this is *my* affair. I'm still waiting for your answer Professor.'

Despite the issues involved, he was quite enjoying this. The two scientists, of course, were playing for identical stakes. Stanyukovitch had his problems too; Steelman could guess the discussions that had taken place at Astrograd and Moscow, and the eagerness with which the Soviet astronauts had grasped this opportunity – which, it must be admitted, they had richly earned.

It was an ironic situation, unimaginable only a dozen years before. Here was NASA and the U.S.S.R. Commission of Astronautics working hand in hand, using him as a pawn for their mutual advantage. He did not resent this, for in their place he would have done the same. But he had no wish to be a pawn; he was an individual who still had some control of his own destiny.

'It's quite true,' said Stanyukovitch, very reluctantly, 'that we can only take a limited number of patients here in Mechnikov. In any case, the station's a research laboratory, not a hospital.'

'How many?' asked Steelman relentlessly.

'Well – fewer than ten,' admitted Stanyukovitch, still more unwillingly.

It was an old problem, of course, though he had never imagined that it would apply to him. From the depths of memory there flashed a newspaper item he had come across long ago. When penicillin had been first discovered, it was so rare that if both Churchill and Roosevelt had been dying for lack of it, only one could have been treated ...

Fewer than ten. He had seen a dozen waiting at Astrograd, and how many were there in the whole world? Once again, as it had done so often in the last few days, the memory of those desolate lovers in the reception room came back to haunt him. Perhaps they were beyond his aid; he would never know.

But one thing he did know. He bore a responsibility that he could not escape. It was true that no man could foresee the future, and the endless consequences of his actions. Yet if it had not been for him, by this time his own country might have had a space hospital circling beyond the atmosphere. How many American lives were upon his conscience? Could he accept the help he had denied to others? Once he might have done so – but not now.

'Gentlemen,' he said, 'I can speak frankly with you both, for I know your interests are identical.' (His mild irony, he saw, did not escape them.) 'I appreciate your help and the trouble you have taken; I am sorry it has been wasted. No – don't protest; this isn't a sudden, quixotic decision on my part. If I was ten years younger, it might be different. Now I feel that this opportunity should be given to someone else – especially in view of my record.' He glanced at Dr. Harkness, who gave an embarrassed smile. 'I also have other personal reasons, and there's no chance that I will change my mind. Please don't think me rude or ungrateful, but I don't wish to discuss the matter any further. Thank you again, and good-bye.'

He broke the circuit; and as the image of the two astonished scientists faded, peace came flooding back into his soul.

Imperceptibly, spring merged into summer. The eagerly awaited Bicentenary celebrations came and went; for the first time in years, he was able to enjoy Independence Day as a private citizen. Now he could sit back and watch the others perform – or he could ignore them if he wished.

Because the ties of a lifetime were too strong to' break, and it would be his last opportunity to see many old friends, he spent hours looking in on both conventions and listening to the commentators. Now that he saw the whole world beneath the light of Eternity, his emotions were no longer involved; he understood the issues and appreciated the arguments, but already he was as detached as an observer from another planet. The tiny, shouting figures on the screen were amusing marionettes, acting out roles in a play that was entertaining, but no longer important – at least, to him.

But it was important to his grandchildren, who would one day move out on to this same stage. He had not forgotten that; they were his share of the future, whatever strange form it might take. And to understand the future, it was necessary to know the past.

He was taking them into that past, as the car swept along Memorial Drive. Diana was at the wheel, with Irene beside her, while he sat with the children, pointing out the familiar sights along the highway. Familiar to him, but not to them; even if they were not old enough to understand all that they were seeing, he hoped they would remember.

Past the marble stillness of Arlington (he thought again of Martin, sleeping on the other side of the world) and up into the hills the car wound its effortless way. Behind them, like a city seen through a mirage, Washington danced and trembled in the summer haze, until the curve of the road hid it from view.

It was quiet at Mount Vernon; there were few visitors so early in the week. As they left the car and walked towards the house, Steelman wondered what the first President of the United States would have thought could he have seen his home as it was today. He could never have dreamed that it would enter its second century still perfectly preserved, a changeless island in the hurrying river of time.

They walked slowly through the beautifully proportioned rooms, doing their best to answer the children's endless questions, trying to assimilate the flavour of an infinitely simpler, infinitely more leisurely mode of life. (But had it seemed simple or leisurely to those who lived it?) It was so hard to imagine a world without electricity, without radio, without any power save that of muscle, wind and water. A world where nothing moved faster than a running horse, and most men died within a few miles of the place where they were born.

The heat, the walking and the incessant questions proved more tiring than Steelman had expected. When they had reached the Music Room, he decided to rest. There were some attractive benches out on the porch, where he could sit in the fresh air and feast his eyes upon the green grass of the lawn.

'Meet me outside,' he explained to Diana, 'when you've done the kitchen and the stables. I'd like to sit down for a while.'

'You're sure you're quite all right?' she said anxiously.

'I never felt better, but I don't want to overdo it. Besides, the kids have drained me dry – I can't think of any more answers. You'll have to invent some; the kitchen's your department, anyway.'

Diana smiled.

'I was never much good in it, was I? But I'll do my best – I don't suppose we'll be more than thirty minutes.'

When they had left him, he walked slowly out on to the lawn. Here Washington must have stood two centuries ago, watching the Potomac wind its way to the sea, thinking of past wars and future problems. And here Martin Steelman, thirty-eighth President of the United States, might have stood a few months hence, had the fates not ruled otherwise.

He could not pretend that he had no regrets, but they were very few. Some men could achieve both power and happiness, but that gift was not for him. Sooner or later, his ambition would have consumed him. In the last few weeks he had known contentment, and for that no price was too great.

He was still marvelling at the narrowness of his escape when his time ran out and Death fell softly from the summer sky.

HATE

ONLY Joey was awake on deck, in the cool stillness before dawn, when the meteor came flaming out of the sky above New Guinea. He watched it climb up the heavens until it passed directly overhead, routing the stars and throwing swift-moving shadows across the crowded deck. The harsh light outlined the bare rigging, the coiled ropes and air hoses, the copper diving helmets neatly snugged down for the night – even the low, pandanus-clad island half a mile away. As it passed into the southwest, out over the emptiness of the Pacific, it began to disintegrate. Incandescent globules broke off, burning and guttering in a trail of fire that stretched a quarter of the way across the sky. It was already dying when it raced out of sight, but Joey did not see its end. Still blazing furiously, it sank below the horizon as if seeking to hurl itself into the face of the hidden sun.

If the sight was spectacular, the utter silence was unnerving. Joey waited and waited and waited, but no sound came from the riven heavens. When, minutes later, there was a sudden splash from the sea close at hand, he gave an involuntary start of surprise – then cursed himself for being frightened by a manta. (A mighty big one, though, to have made so much noise when it jumped.) There was no other sound, and presently he went back to sleep.

In his narrow bunk just aft of the air compressor, Tibor heard nothing. He slept so soundly after his day's work that he had little energy even for dreams – and when they came, they were not the dreams he wanted. In the hours of darkness, as his mind roamed back and forth across the past, it never came to rest amid memories of desire. He had

99

women in Sydney and Brisbane and Darwin and Thursday Island – but none in his dreams. All that he ever remembered when he woke, in the fetid stillness of the cabin, was the dust and fire and blood as the Russian tanks rolled into Budapest. His dreams were not of love, but only of hate.

When Nick shook him back to consciousness, he was dodging the guards on the Austrian border. It took him a few seconds to make the ten-thousand-mile journey to the Great Barrier Reef; then he yawned, kicked away the cockroaches that had been nibbling at his toes and heaved himself out of his bunk.

Breakfast, of course, was the same as always – rice, turtle eggs and bully beef, washed down with strong, sweet tea. The best that could be said of Joey's cooking was that there was plenty of it. Tibor was used to the monotonous diet; he made up for it, and for other deprivations, when he was back on the mainland.

The sun had barely cleared the horizon when the dishes were stacked in the tiny galley and the lugger got under way. Nick sounded cheerful as he took the wheel and headed out from the island; the old pearling-master had every right to be, for the patch of shell they were working was the richest that Tibor had ever seen. With any luck, they would fill their hold in another day or two, and sail back to T. I. with half a ton of shell on board. And then, with a little more luck, he could give up this stinking, dangerous job and get back to civilization. Not that he regretted anything; the Greek had treated him well, and he'd found some good stones when the shells were opened. But he understood now, after nine months on the Reef, why the number of white divers could be counted on the fingers of one hand. Japs and Kanakas and Islanders could take it – but damn few Europeans.

The diesel coughed into silence, and the *Arafura* coasted to rest. They were some two miles from the island, which lay low and green on the water, yet sharply divided from it by its narrow band of dazzling beach. It was no more than a nameless sand bar that a tiny forest had managed to capture, and its only inhabitants were the myriads of stupid muttonbirds that riddled the soft ground with their burrows and made the night hideous with their banshee cries.

There was little talk as the three divers dressed; each man knew what to do, and wasted no time in doing it. As Tibor buttoned on his thick twill jacket, Blanco, his tender, rinsed out the faceplate with vinegar so that it would not become fogged. Then Tibor clambered down the rope ladder, while the heavy helmet and lead corselet were placed over his head. Apart from the jacket, whose padding spread the weight evenly over his shoulders, he was wearing his ordinary clothes. In these warm waters there was no need for rubber suits, and the helmet simply acted as a tiny diving bell held in position by its weight alone. In an emergency the wearer could – if he was lucky – duck out of it and swim back to the surface unhampered. Tibor had seen this done, but he had no wish to try the experiment for himself.

Each time he stood on the last rung of the ladder, gripping his shell bag with one hand and his safety line with the other, the same thought flashed through Tibor's mind. He was leaving the world he knew – but was it for an hour or was it forever? Down there on the sea bed was wealth and death, and one could be sure of neither. The chances were that this would be another day of uneventful drudgery, as were most of the days in the pearl diver's unglamorous life. But Tibor had seen one of his mates die, when his air hose tangled in the *Arafura*'s prop – and he had watched the agony of another whose body twisted with the bends. In the sea, nothing was ever safe or certain. You took your chances with open eyes – and if you lost, there was no point in whining.

He stepped back from the ladder, and the world of sun and sky ceased to exist. Top-heavy with the weight of his helmet, he had to backpedal furiously to keep his body upright. He could see nothing but a featureless blue mist as he sank towards the bottom, and he hoped that Blanco would not play out the safety line too quickly. Swallowing and snorting, he tried to clear his ears as the pressure mounted; the right one 'popped' quickly enough, but a piercing, intolerable pain grew rapidly in the left, which had bothered him for several days. He forced his hand up under the helmet, gripped his nose, and blew with all his might. There was an abrupt, soundless explosion somewhere inside his head, and the pain vanished instantly. He'd have no more trouble on this dive.

Tibor felt the bottom before he saw it. Since he was unable to bend over lest he risk flooding the open helmet, his vision in the downward direction was very limited. He could see around, but not immediately below. What he did see was reassuring in its drab monotony – gently undulating, muddy plain that faded out of sight about ten feet ahead. A yard to his left a tiny fish was nibbling at a piece of coral the size and shape of a lady's fan. That was all; there was no beauty, no underwater fairyland here. But there was money, and that was what mattered.

The safety line gave a gentle pull as the lugger started to drift downward, moving broadside-on across the patch, and Tibor began to walk forward with the springy, slow-motion step forced on him by weightlessness and water resistance. As Number Two diver he was working from the bow; amidships was Stephen, still comparatively inexperienced, while at the stern was the head diver, Billy. The three men seldom saw each other while they were working; each had his own lane to search as the *Arafura* drifted silently before the wind. Only at the extremes of the zig-zags might they sometimes glimpse one another as dim shapes looming through the mist.

It needed a trained eye to spot the shells beneath their camouflage of algae and weeds, but often the molluscs betrayed themselves. When they felt the vibrations of the approaching diver, they would snap shut – and there would be a momentary, nacreous flicker in the gloom. Yet even then they sometimes escaped, for the moving ship might drag the diver past before he could collect the prize just out of reach. In the early days of his apprenticeship, Tibor had missed quite a few of the big silver lips – any one of which might have contained some fabulous pearl. Or so he had imagined, before the glamour of the profession had worn off, and he realized that pearls were so rare that you might as well forget them. The most valuable stone he'd ever brought up had been sold for fifty-six dollars, and the shell he gathered on a good morning was worth more than that. If the industry had depended on gems instead of mother-of-pearl, it would have gone broke years ago.

There was no sense of time in this world of mist. You walked beneath the invisible, drifting ship, with the throb of the air compressor pounding in your ears, the green haze moving past your eyes. At long intervals you would spot a shell, wrench it from the sea bed, and drop it in your bag. If you were lucky, you might gather a couple of dozen on a single drift across the patch; on the other hand, you might not find a single one.

You were alert for danger, but not worried by it. The real risks were simple, unspectacular things like tangled air hoses or safety lines – not sharks, groupers or octopuses. Sharks ran when they saw your air bubbles, and in all his hours of diving Tibor had seen just one octopus, every bit of two feet across. As for groupers – well, *they* were to be taken seriously, for they could swallow a diver at one gulp if they felt hungry enough. But there was little chance of meeting them on this flat and desolate plain; there was none of the coral caves in which they could make their homes.

The shock would not have been so great, therefore, if this uniform, level greyness had not lulled him into a sense of security. At one moment he was walking steadily towards an unreachable wall of mist, which retreated as fast as he approached. And then without warning, his private nightmare was looming above him.

Tibor hated spiders, and there was a certain creature in the sea that seemed deliberately contrived to take advantage of that phobia. He had never met one, and his mind had always shied away from the thought of such an encounter, but Tibor knew that the Japanese spider crab can span twelve feet across its spindly legs. That it was harmless mattered not in the least; a spider as big as a man simply had no right to exist.

As soon as he saw that cage of slender, joined limbs emerge from the all-encompassing greyness, Tibor began to scream with uncontrollable terror. He never remembered jerking his safety line, but Blanco reacted with the instantaneous perception of the ideal tender. His helmet still echoing to his screams, Tibor felt himself snatched from the sea bed, lifted towards light and air – and sanity. As he swept upwards, he saw both the strangeness and the absurdity of his mistake, and regained a measure of control. But he was still trembling so violently when Blanco lifted off his helmet that it was some time before he could speak.

'What the hell's going on here?' demanded Nick. 'Everyone knocking off work early?'

It was then that Tibor realized that he was not the first to come up. Stephen was sitting amidships, smoking a cigarette and looking completely unconcerned. The stern diver, doubtless wondering what had happened was being hauled up willy-nilly by his tender, since the *Arafura* had come to rest and all operations had been suspended until the trouble was resolved.

'There's some kind of wreck down there,' said Tibor. 'I ran right into it. All I could see were a lot of wires and rods.'

To his annoyance and self-contempt, the memory set him trembling again.

'Don't see why *that* should give you the shakes,' grumbled Nick. Nor could Tibor; here on this sun-drenched deck, it was impossible to explain how a harmless shape glimpsed through the mist could set one's whole mind jangling with terror.

'I nearly got hung up on it,' he lied. 'Blanco pulled me clear just in time.'

'Hmm,' said Nick obviously not convinced. 'Anyway, it ain't a ship.' He gestured towards the midships diver. 'Steve ran into a mess of ropes and cloth – like thick nylon, he says. Sounds like some kind of parachute.' The old Greek stared in disgust at the soggy stump of his cigar, then flicked it overboard. 'Soon as Billy's up, we'll go back and take a look. Might be worth something – remember what happened to Jo Chambers.'

Tibor remembered; the story was famous the whole length of the Great Barrier Reef. Jo had been a lone-wolf fisherman who, in the last months of the war had spotted a DC-3 lying in shallow water a few miles off the Queensland coast. After prodigies of singlehanded salvage, he had broken into the fuselage and started unloading boxes of taps and dies, perfectly protected by their greased wrappings. For a while he had run a flourishing import business, but when the police caught up with him he reluctantly revealed his source of supply; Australian cops can be very persuasive.

And it was then, after weeks and weeks of backbreaking underwater work, that Jo discovered what his DC-3 had been carrying besides the miserable few hundred quid's worth of tools he had been flogging to garages and work-shops on the mainland. The big wooden crates he'd never got round to opening held a week's payroll for the U.S. Pacific forces – most of it in twenty-dollar gold pieces.

No such luck here, thought Tibor as he sank over the side again; but the aircraft – or whatever it was – might contain valuable instruments, and there could be a reward for its discovery. Besides, he owed it to himself; he wanted to see exactly what it was that had given him such a fright.

Ten minutes later, he knew it was no aircraft. It was the wrong shape and it was much too small – only about twenty feet long and half that in width. Here and there on the gently tapering body were access hatches and tiny ports through which unknown instruments peered at the world. It seemed unharmed, though one end had been fused as if by terrific heat. From the other sprouted a tangle of antennas, all of them broken or bent by the impact with the water. Even now they bore an incredible resemblance to the legs of a giant insect.

Tibor was no fool; he guessed at once what the thing was. Only one problem remained, and he solved that with little difficulty. Though they had been partly charred away by heat, stencilled words could still be read on some of the hatch covers. The letters were Cyrillic, and Tibor knew enough Russian to pick out references to electrical supplies and pressurizing systems.

'So they've lost a sputnik' he told himself with satisfaction. He could imagine what had happened; the thing had come down too fast, and in the wrong place. Around one end were the tattered remnants of flotation bags; they had burst under the impact, and the vehicle had sunk like a stone. The *Arafura*'s crew would have to apologize to Joey; he hadn't been drinking grog. What he'd seen burning across the stars must have been the rocket carrier, separated from its pay load and falling back unchecked into the Earth's atmosphere.

For a long time Tibor hovered on the sea bed, knees bent in the diver's crouch as he regarded this space creature now trapped in an alien element. His mind was full of half-formed plans but none had yet come clearly into focus. He no longer cared about the salvage money; much more important were the prospects of revenge. Here was one of the proudest creations of Soviet technology – and Szabo Tibor, late of Budapest, was the only man on earth who knew.

There must be some way of exploiting the situation – of doing harm to the country and the cause he now hated with such smouldering intensity. In his waking hours, he was seldom conscious of the hate, and still less did he ever stop to analyse its real cause. Here in this lonely world of sea and sky, of steaming mangrove swamps and dazzling coral strands, there was nothing to recall the past. Yet he could never escape it, and sometimes the demons in his mind would awake, lashing him into a fury of rage or vicious, wanton destructiveness. So far he had been lucky; he had not killed anyone. But some day . . .

An anxious jerk from Blanco interrupted his reveries of vengeance. He gave a reassuring signal to his tender, and started a closer examination of the capsule. What did it weigh? Could it be hoisted easily? There were many things he had to discover, before he could settle on any definite plans.

He braced himself against the corrugated metal wall, and pushed cautiously. There was a definite movement as the capsule rocked on the sea bed. Maybe it could be lifted, even with the few pieces of tackle that the *Arafura* could muster. It was probably lighter than it looked.

Tibor pressed his helmet against a flat section of the hull and listened intently. He had half expected to hear some mechanical noise, such as the whirring of electric motors.

Instead, there was utter silence. With the hilt of his knife, he rapped sharply on the metal, trying to gauge its thickness and to locate any weak spots. On the third try, he got results: but they were not what he had anticipated.

In a furious, desperate tattoo, the capsule rapped back at him.

Until this moment, Tibor had never dreamed that there might be someone inside; the capsule had seemed far too small. Then he realized that he had been thinking in terms of conventional aircraft; there was plenty of room here for a little pressure cabin in which a dedicated astronaut could spend a few cramped hours.

As a kaleidoscope can change its pattern completely in a single moment, so the half-formed plans in Tibor's mind dissolved and then crystallized into a new shape. Behind the thick glass of his helmet, he ran his tongue lightly across his lips. If Nick could have seen him now, he would have wondered – as he had sometimes done before – whether his Number Two diver was wholly sane. Gone were all thoughts of a remote and impersonal vengeance against something as abstract as a nation or a machine; now it would be man to man.

'Took your time, didn't you?' said Nick. 'What did you find?'

'It's Russian,' said Tibor. 'Some kind of sputnik. If we can get a rope around it, I think we can lift it off the bottom. But it's too heavy to get aboard.'

Nick chewed thoughtfully on his eternal cigar. The pearling master was worried about a point that had not occurred to Tibor. If there were any salvage operations around here, everyone would know where the *Arafura* had been drifting. When the news got back to Thursday Island, his private patch of shell would be cleaned out in no time.

They'd have to keep quiet about the whole affair, or else

108

haul the damn thing up themselves and not say where they'd found it. Whatever happened, it looked like being more of a nuisance than it was worth. Nick, who shared most Australians' profound suspicion of authority, had already decided that all he'd get for his trouble would be a nice letter of thanks.

'The boys won't go down,' he said. 'They think it's a bomb. Want to leave it alone.'

'Tell 'em not to worry,' replied Tibor. 'I'll handle it.' He tried to keep his voice normal and unemotional but this was too good to be true. If the other divers heard the tapping from the capsule, his plans would have been frustrated.

He gestured to the island, green and lovely on the skyline.

'Only one thing we can do. If we can heave it a couple of feet off the bottom, we can run for the shore. Once we're in shallow water, it won't be too hard to haul it up on the beach. We can use the boats, and maybe get a block and tackle on one of those trees.'

Nick considered the idea without much enthusiasm. He doubted if they could get the sputnik through the reef, even on the leeward side of the island, but he was all in favour of lugging it away from this patch of shell; they could always dump it somewhere else, buoy the place, and still get whatever credit was going.

'O.K.,' he said. 'Down you go. That two-inch rope's the strongest we've got – better take that. Don't be all the bloody day; we've lost enough time already.'

Tibor had no intention of being all day. Six hours would be quite long enough. That was one of the first things he had learned, from the signals through the wall.

It was a pity that he could not hear the Russian's voice; but the Russian could hear him, and that was what really mattered. When he pressed his helmet against the metal and shouted, most of his words got through. So far, it had been a friendly conversation; Tibor had no intention of showing his hand until the right psychological moment.

The first move had been to establish a code – one knock for 'yes', two for 'no'. After that, it was merely a matter of framing suitable questions; given time, there was no fact or idea that could not be communicated by means of these two signals. It would have been a much tougher job if Tibor had been forced to use his indifferent Russian; he had been pleased, but not surprised, to find that the trapped pilot understood English perfectly.

There was air in the capsule for another five hours; the occupant was uninjured; yes, the Russians knew where it had come down. That last reply gave Tibor pause. Perhaps the pilot was lying, but it might very well be true. Although something had obviously gone wrong with the planned return to Earth, the tracking ships out in the Pacific must have located the impact point – with what accuracy, he could not guess. Still, did that matter? It might take them days to get here, even if they came racing straight into Australian territorial waters without bothering to get permission from Canberra. He was master of the situation; the entire might of the U.S.S.R. could do nothing to interfere with his plans – until it was much too late.

The heavy rope fell in coils on the sea bed, stirring up a cloud of silt that drifted like smoke down the slow current. Now that the sun was higher in the sky, the underwater world was no longer wrapped in a grey, twilight gloom. The sea bed was colourless but bright, and the boundary of vision was now almost fifteen feet away. For the first time, Tibor could see the space capsule in its entirety. It was such a peculiar-looking object, being designed for conditions beyond all normal experience, that there was an eye-teasing wrongness about it. One searched in vain for a front or a rear; there was no way of telling us what direction it pointed as it sped along its orbit.

Tibor pressed his helmet against the metal and shouted.

'I'm back,' he called. 'Can you hear me?'

Tap

'I've got a rope, and I'm going to tie it on to the para-chute cables. We're about three kilometres from an island, and as soon as we've made you fast we'll head towards it. We can't lift you out of the water with the gear on the lugger, so we'll try to get you up on the beach. You under-stand?'

Tap

It took only a few moments to secure the rope; now he had better get clear before the *Arafura* started to lift. But there was something he had to do first.

'Hello!' he shouted. 'I've fixed the rope. We'll lift in a minute. D'you hear me?'

Tap

'Then you can hear this too. You'll never get there alive. I've fixed *that* as well.'

Tap, tap

'You've got five hours to die. My brother took longer than that, when he ran into your mine field. You under-stand? I'm from Budapest. I hate you and your country and everything it stands for. You've taken my home, my family, made my people slaves. I wish I could see your face now – I wish I could watch you die, as I had to watch Theo. When you're halfway to the island, this rope is going to break where I cut it, I'll go down and fix another – and that'll break, too. You can sit in there and wait for the bumps.'

Tibor stopped abruptly, shaken and exhausted by the violence of his emotion. There was no room for logic or reason in this orgasm of hate; he did not pause to think, for he dared not. Yet somewhere far down inside his mind the real truth was burning its way up towards the light of con-sciousness.

It was not the Russians he hated, for all that they had done. It was himself, for he had done more. The blood of Theo, and of ten thousand countrymen, was upon his own hands. No one could have been a better Communist than he had been, or have more supinely believed the propaganda from Moscow. At school and college, he had been the first to hunt out and denounce 'traitors'. (How many had he sent to the labour camps or the AVO torture chambers?) When he had seen the truth, it was far, far too late; and even then, he had not fought – he had run.

He had run across the world, trying to escape his guilt; and the two drugs of danger and dissipation had helped him to forget the past. The only pleasures life gave him now were the loveless embraces he sought so feverishly when he was on the mainland, and his present mode of existence was proof that these were not enough. If he now had the power to deal out death, it was only because he had come here in search of it himself.

There was no sound from the capsule; its silence seemed contemptuous, mocking. Angrily, Tibor banged against it with the hilt of his knife.

'Did you hear me?' he shouted. 'Did you hear me?'

No answer.

'Damn you! I know you're listening! If you don't answer, I'll hole you and let the water in!'

He was sure that he could, with the sharp point of his knife. But that was the last thing he wanted to do; that would be too quick, too easy an ending.

There was still no sound; maybe the Russian had fainted. Tibor hoped not, but there was no point in waiting any longer. He gave a vicious parting bang on the capsule, and signalled to his tender.

Nick had news for him when he broke the surface.

'T. I. radio's been squawking,' he said. 'The Ruskies are asking everyone to look out for one of their rockets. They say it should be floating somewhere off the Queensland coast. Sounds as if they want it badly.'

'Did they say anything else about it?' Tibor asked anxiously.

'Oh yes – it's been round the moon a couple of times.'

'That all?'

'Nothing else that I remember. There was a lot of science stuff I didn't get.'

That figured; it was just like the Russians to keep as quiet as they could about an experiment that had gone wrong.

'You tell T. I. that we'd found it?'

'Are you crazy? Anyway, the radio's crook; couldn't if we wanted to. Fixed that rope properly?'

'Yes – see if you can haul her off the bottom.'

The end of the rope had been wound round the mainmast, and in a few seconds it had been drawn taut. Although the sea was calm, there was a slight swell, and the lugger was rolling ten or fifteen degrees. With each roll, the gunwales would rise a couple of feet, then drop again. There was a lift here of several tons, but one had to be careful in using it.

The rope twanged, the woodwork groaned and creaked, and for a moment Tibor was afraid that the weakened line would part too soon. But it held, and the load lifted. They got a further hoist on the second roll – and on the third. Then the capsule was clear of the sea bed, and the *Arafura* was listing slightly to port.

'Let's go,' said Nick, taking the wheel. 'Should be able to get her half a mile before she bumps again.'

The lugger began to move slowly towards the island, carrying its hidden burden beneath it. As he leaned on the rails, letting the sun steam the moisture from his sodden clothing, Tibor felt at peace for the first time in – how many months? Even his hate had ceased to burn like fire in his

113

brain. Perhaps, like love, it was a passion that could never be satisfied; but for the moment, at least, it was satiated.

There was no weakening of his resolve; he was implacably set upon the vengeance that had been so strangely – so miraculously – placed within his power. Blood called for blood, and now the ghosts that haunted him might rest at last. Yet he felt a strange sympathy, even pity, towards the unknown man through whom he could now strike back at the enemies who had once been his friends. He was robbing them of much more than a single life – for what was one man, even a highly trained scientist – to the Russians? What he was taking from them was power and prestige and knowledge, the things they valued most.

He began to worry when they were two thirds of the way to the island, and the rope had not parted. There was still four hours to go, and that was much too long. For the first time it occurred to him that his entire plan might miscarry, and might even recoil on his head. Suppose that, despite everything, Nick managed to get the capsule up on the beach before the deadline?

With a deep 'twang' that set the whole ship vibrating, the rope came snaking out of the water, scattering spray in all directions.

'Might have guessed,' muttered Nick. 'She was just starting to bump. You like to go down again, or shall I send one of the boys?'

'I'll take it,' Tibor hastily answered. 'I can do it quicker than they can.'

That was perfectly true, but it took him twenty minutes to locate the capsule. The *Arafura* had drifted well away from it before Nick could stop the engine, and there was a time when Tibor wondered if he would ever find it again. He quartered the sea bed in great arcs, and it was not until he had accidentally tangled in the trailing parachute that his search was ended. The shrouds lay pulsating slowly in the current like some weird and hideous marine monster – but there was nothing that Tibor feared now except frustration, and his pulse barely quickened as he saw the whitely looming mass ahead.

The capsule was scratched and stained with mud, but appeared undamaged. It was lying on its side now, looking rather like a giant milk churn that had been tipped over. The passenger must have been bumped around, but if he'd fallen all the way back from the moon, he must have been well padded and was probably still in good shape. Tibor hoped so; it would be a pity if the remaining three hours were wasted.

Once again he rested the verdigrised copper of his helmet against the no-longer-quite-so-brightly-gleaming metal of the capsule.

'Hello!' he shouted. 'Can you hear me?'

Perhaps the Russian would try to balk him by remaining silent – but that, surely, was asking too much of any man's self-control. Tibor was right; almost at once there was the sharp knock of the reply.

'So glad you're there,' he called back. 'Things are working out just the way I said, though I guess I'll have to cut the rope a little deeper.'

The capsule did not answer. It never answered again, though Tibor banged and banged on the next dive – and on the next. But he hardly expected it to then, for they'd had to stop for a couple of hours to ride out a squall, and the time limit had expired long before he made his final descent. He was a little annoyed about that, for he had planned a farewell message. He shouted it just the same, though he knew he was wasting his breath.

By early afternoon, the *Arafura* had come in as close as she dared. There were only a few feet of water beneath her, and the tide was falling. The capsule broke surface at the bottom of each wave trough, and was now firmly stranded on a sandbank. There was no hope of moving it any farther; it was stuck, until a high sea would dislodge it.

Nick regarded the situation with an expert eye.

'There's a six-foot tide tonight,' he said. 'The way she's lying now, she'll be in only a couple of feet of water at low. We'll be able to get at her with the boats.'

They waited off the sandbank while the sun and the tide went down, and the radio broadcast intermittent reports of a search that was coming closer but still far away. Late in the afternoon the capsule was almost clear of the water; the crew rowed the small boat towards it with a reluctance which Tibor, to his annoyance, found himself sharing.

'It's got a door in the side,' said Nick suddenly. 'Jeeze – think there's anyone in it?'

'Could be,' answered Tibor, his voice not as steady as he thought. Nick glanced at him curiously. His diver had been acting strangely all day, but he knew better than to ask him what was wrong. In this part of the world, you soon learned to mind your own business.

The boat, rocking slightly in the choppy sea, had now come alongside the capsule. Nick reached out and grabbed one of the twisted antenna stubs; then, with catlike agility, he clambered up the curved metal surface. Tibor made no attempt to follow him, but watched silently from the boat as he examined the entrance hatch.

'Unless it's jammed,' Nick muttered, 'there must be some way of opening it from outside. Just our luck if it needs special tools.'

His fears were groundless. The word 'Open' had been stencilled in ten languages around the recessed door catch, and it took only seconds to deduce its mode of operation. As the air hissed out, Nick said 'Phew!' and turned suddenly pale. He looked at Tibor as if seeking support, but Tibor avoided his eye. Then, reluctantly, Nick lowered himself into the capsule.

He was gone for a long time. At first, they could hear muffled bangings and bumpings from the inside, followed by a string of bilingual profanity. And then there was a silence that went on and on and on.

When at last Nick's head appeared above the hatchway, his leathery, wind-tanned face was grey and streaked with tears. As Tibor saw this incredible sight, he felt a sudden ghastly premonition. Something had gone horribly wrong, but his mind was too numb to anticipate the truth. It came soon enough, when Nick handed down his burden, no larger than an over-sized doll.

Blanco took it, as Tibor shrank to the stern of the boat. As he looked at the calm, waxen face, fingers of ice seemed to close not only upon his heart, but around his loins. In the same moment, both hate and desire died forever within him, as he knew the price of his revenge.

The dead astronaut was perhaps more beautiful in death than she had been in life; tiny though she was, she must have been tough as well as highly trained to qualify for this mission. As she lay at Tibor's feet, she was neither a Russian nor the first human being to have seen the far side of the moon; she was merely the girl that he had killed.

Nick was talking, from a long way off.

'She was carrying this,' he said, in an unsteady voice. 'Had it tight in her hand – took me a long time to get it out.'

Tibor scarcely heard him, and never even glanced at the tiny spool of tape lying in Nick's palm. He could not guess, in this moment beyond all feeling, that the Furies had yet to close in upon his soul – and that soon the whole world would be listening to an accusing voice from beyond the grave, branding him more irrevocably than any man since Cain.

SUNJAMMER

THE enormous disc of sail strained at its rigging, already filled with the wind that blew between the worlds. In three minutes the race would begin, yet now John Merton felt more relaxed, more at peace, than at any time for the past year. Whatever happened when the Commodore gave the starting signal, whether *Diana* carried him to victory or defeat, he had achieved his ambition. After a lifetime spent in designing ships for others, now he would sail his own.

'T minus two minutes,' said the cabin radio. 'Please confirm your readiness.'

One by one, the other skippers answered. Merton recognized all the voices – some tense, some calm – for they were the voices of his friends and rivals. On the four inhabited worlds, there were scarcely twenty men who could sail a sun-yacht; and they were all here, on the starting-line or aboard the escort vessels, orbiting twenty-two thousand miles above the equator.

'Number One, *Gossamer* – ready to go.'

'Number Two, *Santa Maria* – all O.K.'

'Number Three, *Sunbeam* – O.K.'

'Number Four, *Woomera* – all systems go.'

Merton smiled at that last echo from the early, primitive days of astronautics. But it had become part of the tradition of space; and there were times when a man needed to evoke the shades of those who had gone before him to the stars.

'Number Five, *Lebedev* – we're ready.'

'Number Six, *Arachne* – O.K.'

Now it was his turn, at the end of the line; strange to

think that the words he was speaking in this tiny cabin were being heard by at least five billion people.

'Number Seven, *Diana* – ready to start.'

'One through Seven acknowledged.' The voice from the judge's launch was impersonal. 'Now T minus one minute.'

Merton scarcely heard it; for the last time, he was checking the tension in the rigging. The needles of all the dynamometers were steady; the immense sail was taut, its mirror surface sparkling and glittering gloriously in the sun.

To Merton, floating weightless at the periscope, it seemed to fill the sky. As well it might – for out there were fifty million square feet of sail, linked to his capsule by almost a hundred miles of rigging. All the canvas of all the tea-clippers that had once raced like clouds across the China seas, sewn into one gigantic sheet, could not match the single sail that *Diana* had spread beneath the sun. Yet it was little more substantial than a soap-bubble; that two square miles of aluminized plastic was only a few millionths of an inch thick.

'T minus ten seconds. All recording cameras *on.*'

Something so huge, yet so frail, was hard for the mind to grasp. And it was harder still to realize that this fragile mirror could tow them free of Earth, merely by the power of the sunlight it would trap.

'... Five, four, three, two, one, *cut!*'

Seven knife-blades sliced through the seven thin lines tethering the yachts to the mothership that had assembled and serviced them.

Until this moment, all had been circling Earth together in a rigidly held formation, but now the yachts would begin to disperse, like dandelion seeds drifting before the breeze. And the winner would be the one that first drifted past the Moon.

Aboard *Diana*, nothing seemed to be happening. But Merton knew better; though his body could feel no thrust, the instrument board told him he was now accelerating at almost one thousandth of a gravity. For a rocket, that figure would have been ludicrous – but this was the first time any solar yacht had attained it. *Diana*'s design was sound; the vast sail was living up to his calculations. At this rate, two circuits of the Earth would build up his speed to escape velocity – then he could head out for the Moon, with the full force of the Sun behind him.

The full force of the Sun. He smiled wryly, remembering all his attempts to explain solar sailing to those lecture audiences back on Earth. That had been the only way he could raise money, in those early days. He might be Chief Designer of Cosmodyne Corporation, with a whole string of successful spaceships to his credit, but his firm had not been exactly enthusiastic about his hobby.

'Hold your hands out to the Sun,' he'd said. 'What do you feel? Heat, of course. But there's pressure as well – though you've never noticed it, because it's so tiny. Over the area of your hands, it only comes to about a millionth of an ounce.

'But out in space, even a pressure as small as that can be important – for it's acting all the time, hour after hour, day after day. Unlike rocket fuel, it's free and unlimited. If we want to, we can use it; we can build sails to catch the radiation blowing from the Sun.'

At that point, he would pull out a few square yards of sail material and toss it towards the audience. The silvery film would coil and twist like smoke, then drift slowly to the ceiling in the hot-air currents.

'You can see how light it is,' he'd continue. 'A square mile weighs only a ton, and can collect five pounds of radiation pressure. So it will start moving – and we can let it tow us along, if we attach rigging to it.

'Of course, its acceleration will be tiny – about a thousandth of a g. That doesn't seem much, but let's see what it means.

'It means that in the first second, we'll move about a fifth of an inch. I suppose a healthy snail could do better than that. But after a minute, we've covered sixty feet, and will be doing just over a mile an hour. That's not bad, for something driven by pure sunlight! After an hour, we're forty miles from our starting point, and will be moving at eighty miles an hour. Please remember that in space there's no friction, so once you start anything moving, it will keep going forever. You'll be surprised when I tell you what our thousandth-of-a-g sailing boat will be doing at the end of a day's run. *Almost two thousand miles an hour!* If it starts from orbit – as it has to, of course – it can reach escape velocity in a couple of days. And all without burning a single drop of fuel!'

Well, he'd convinced them, and in the end he'd even convinced Cosmodyne. Over the last twenty years, a new sport had come into being. It had been called the sport of billionaires, and that was true – but it was beginning to pay for itself in terms of publicity and television coverage. The prestige of four continents and two worlds was riding on this race, and it had the biggest audience in history.

Diana had made a good start; time to take a look at the opposition. Moving very gently. Though there were shock absorbers between the control capsule and the delicate rigging, he was determined to run no risk. Merton stationed himself at the periscope.

There they were, looking like strange silver flowers planted in the dark fields of space. The nearest, South America's *Santa Maria*, was only fifty miles away; it bore a resemblance to a boy's kite – but a kite more than a mile on its side. Farther away, the University of Astrograd's *Lebedev* looked like a Maltese cross; the sails that formed the four arms could apparently be tilted for steering purposes. In contrast, the Federation of Australasia's *Woomera* was a simple parachute, four miles in circumference. General Spacecraft's *Arachne*, as its name suggested, looked like a spider-web – and had been built on the same principles, by robot shuttles spiralling out from a central point. Eurospace Corporation's *Gossamer* was an identical design, on a slightly smaller scale. And the Republic of Mars' *Sunbeam* was a flat ring, with a half-mile-wide hole in the centre, spinning slowly so that centrifugal force gave it stiffness. That was an old idea, but no one had ever made it work. Merton was fairly sure that the colonials would be in trouble when they started to turn.

That would not be for another six hours, when the yachts had moved along the first quarter of their slow and stately twenty-four hour orbit. Here at the beginning of the race, they were all heading directly away from the Sun – running, as it were, before the solar wind. One had to make the most of this lap, before the boats swung round to the other side of Earth and then started to head back into the Sun.

Time for the first check, Merton told himself, while he had no navigational worries. With the periscope, he made a careful examination of the sail, concentrating on the points where the rigging was attached to it. The shroud-lines – narrow bands of unsilvered plastic film – would have been completely invisible had they not been coated with fluorescent paint. Now they were taut lines of coloured light, dwindling away for hundreds of yards towards that gigantic sail. Each had its own electric windlass, not much bigger than a game-fisherman's reel. The little windlasses were continually turning, playing lines in or out, as the autopilot kept the sail trimmed at the correct angle to the Sun.

The play of sunlight on the great flexible mirror was beautiful to watch. It was undulating in slow, stately oscillations, sending multiple images of the Sun marching across the heavens, until they faded away at the edges of the sail. Such leisurely vibrations were to be expected in this vast and flimsy structure; they were usually quite harmless, but Merton watched them carefully. Sometimes they could build up to the catastrophic undulations known as the wriggles, which could tear a sail to pieces.

When he was satisfied that everything was shipshape, he swept the periscope around the sky, rechecking the positions of his rivals. It was as he had hoped; the weeding-out process had begun, as the less efficient boats fell astern. But the real test would come when they passed into the shadow of the Earth; then manoeuvrability would count as much as speed.

It seemed a strange thing to do, now that the race had just started, but it might be a good idea to get some sleep. The two man crews on the other boats could take it in turns, but Merton had no one to relieve him. He must rely on his physical resources – like that other solitary seaman Joshua Slocum, in his tiny *Spray*. The American skipper had sailed *Spray* single-handed round the world; he could never have dreamt that, two centuries later, a man would be sailing single-handed from Earth to Moon – inspired, at least partly, by his example.

Merton snapped the elastic bands of the cabin seat around his waist and legs, then placed the electrodes of the sleep-inducer on his forehead. He set the timer for three hours, and relaxed.

Very gently, hypnotically, the electronic pulses throbbed in the frontal lobes of his brain. Coloured spirals of light expanded beneath his closed eyelids, widening outwards to infinity. Then – nothing ...

The brazen clamour of the alarm dragged him back from his dreamless sleep. He was instantly awake, his eyes scanning the instrument panel. Only two hours had passed – but above the accelerometer, a red light was flashing. Thrust was falling; *Diana* was losing power.

Merton's first thought was that something had happened to the sail; perhaps the antispin devices had failed, and the rigging had become twisted. Swiftly, he checked the meters that showed the tension in the shroud-lines. Strange, on one side of the sail they were reading normally – but on the other, the pull was dropping slowly even as he watched.

In sudden understanding, Merton grabbed the periscope, switched to wide-angle vision, and started to scan the edge of the sail. Yes – there was the trouble, and it could have only one cause.

A huge, sharp-edged shadow had begun to slide across the gleaming silver of the sail. Darkness was falling upon *Diana*, as if a cloud had passed between her and the Sun. And in the dark, robbed of the rays that drove her, she would lose all thrust and drift helplessly through space.

But, of course, there were no clouds here, more than twenty thousand miles above Earth. If there was a shadow, it must be made by man.

Merton grinned as he swung the periscope towards the Sun, switching on the filters that would allow him to look full into its blazing face without being blinded.

'Manoeuvre 4a,' he muttered to himself. 'We'll see who can play best at *that* game.'

It looked as if a giant planet was crossing the face of the Sun. A great black disc had bitten deep into its edge. Twenty miles astern, *Gossamer* was trying to arrange an artificial eclipse – specially for *Diana*'s benefit.

The manoeuvre was a perfectly legitimate one; back in the days of ocean racing, skippers had often tried to rob each other of the wind. With any luck, you could leave your rival becalmed, with his sails collapsing around him – and be well ahead before he could undo the damage.

Merton had no intention of being caught so easily. There was plenty of time to take evasive action; things happened very slowly, when you were running a solar sailingboat. It would be at least twenty minutes before *Gossamer* could slide completely across the face of the Sun, and leave him in darkness.

Diana's tiny computer – the size of a matchbox, but the equivalent of a thousand human mathematicians – considered the problem for a full second and then flashed the answer. He'd have to open control panels three and four, until the sail had developed an extra twenty degrees of tilt; then the radiation pressure would blow him out of *Gossamer*'s dangerous shadow, back into the full blast of the Sun. It was a pity to interfere with the auto-pilot, which had been carefully programmed to give the fastest possible run – but that, after all, was why he was here. This was what made solar yachting a sport, rather than a battle between computers.

Out went control lines one to six, slowly undulating like sleepy snakes as they momentarily lost their tension. Two miles away, the triangular panels began to open lazily, spilling sunlight through the sail. Yet, for a long time, nothing seemed to happen. It was hard to grow accustomed to this slow motion world, where it took minutes for the effects of any action to become visible to the eye. Then Merton saw that the sail was indeed tipping towards the Sun – and that *Gossamer*'s shadow was sliding harmlessly away, its cone of darkness lost in the deeper night of space.

Long before the shadow had vanished, and the disc of the Sun had cleared again, he reversed the tilt and brought *Diana* back on course. Her new momentum would carry her clear of the danger; no need to overdo it, and upset his calculations by side-stepping too far. That was another rule that was hard to learn. The very moment you had started something happening in space, it was already time to think about stopping it.

He reset the alarm, ready for the next natural or man-made emergency; perhaps *Gossamer*, or one of the other contestants, would try the same trick again. Meanwhile, it was time to eat, though he did not feel particularly hungry. One used little physical energy in space, and it was easy to forget about food. Easy – and dangerous; for when an emergency arose, you might not have the reserves needed to deal with it.

He broke open the first of the meal packets, and inspected it without enthusiasm. The name on the label – SPACE-TASTIES – was enough to put him off. And he had grave doubts about the promise printed underneath. Guaranteed Crumbless. It had been said that crumbs were a greater danger to space vehicles than meteorites. They could drift into the most unlikely places, causing short circuits, blocking vital jets and getting into instruments that were supposed to be hermetically sealed.

Still, the liverwurst went down pleasantly enough; so did the chocolate and the pineapple puree. The plastic coffee-bulb was warming on the electric heater when the outside world broke in on his solitude. The radio operator on the Commodore's launch routed a call to him.

'Dr. Merton? If you can spare the time, Jeremy Blair would like a few words with you.' Blair was one of the more responsible news commentators, and Merton had been on his programme many times. He could refuse to be interviewed, of course, but he liked Blair, and at the moment he could certainly not claim to be too busy. 'I'll take it,' he answered.

'Hello, Dr. Merton,' said the commentator immediately, 'Glad you can spare a few minutes. And congratulations – you seem to be ahead of the field.'

'Too early in the game to be sure of that,' Merton answered cautiously.

'Tell me, doctor – why did you decide to sail *Diana* by yourself? Just because it's never been done before?'

'Well, isn't that a very good reason? But it wasn't the only one, of course.' He paused, choosing his words carefully. 'You know how critically the performance of a sun-yacht depends on its mass. A second man, with all his supplies, would mean another five hundred pounds. That could easily be the difference between winning and losing.'

'And you're quite certain that you can handle *Diana* alone?'

'Reasonably sure, thanks to the automatic controls I've designed. My main job is to supervise and make decisions.'

'But – two square miles of sail! It just doesn't seem possible for one man to cope with all that!'

Merton laughed.

'Why not? Those two square miles produce maximum pull of just ten pounds. I can exert more force with my little finger.'

'Well, thank you, doctor. And good luck.'

As the commentator signed off, Merton felt a little ashamed of himself. For his answer had been only part of the truth; and he was sure that Blair was shrewd enough to know it.

There was just one reason why he was here, alone in space. For almost forty years he had worked with teams of hundreds or even thousands of men, helping to design the most complex vehicles that the world had ever seen. For the last twenty years he had led one of those teams, and watched his creations go soaring to the stars. (But there were failures that he could never forget, even though the faults had not been his.) He was famous, with a successful career behind him. Yet he had never done anything by himself; always he had been one of an army.

This was his very last chance of individual achievement, and he would share it with no one. There would be no more solar yachting for at least five years, as the period of the quiet Sun ended and the cycle of bad weather began, with radiation storms bursting through the Solar System. When it was safe again for these frail, unshielded craft to venture aloft, he would be too old. If, indeed, he was not too old already . . .

He dropped the empty food containers into the waste disposal, and turned once more to the periscope. At first, he could find only five of the other yachts; there was no sign of *Woomera*. It took him several minutes to locate her – a dim, star-eclipsing phantom, neatly caught in the shadow of *Lebedev*. He could imagine the frantic efforts the Australasians were making to extricate themselves, and wondered how they had fallen into the trap. It suggested that *Lebedev* was unusually manoeuvrable; she would bear watching, though she was too far away to menace *Diana* at the moment.

Now the Earth had almost vanished. It had waned to a narrow, brilliant bow of light that was moving steadily towards the Sun. Dimly outlined within that burning bow was the night side of the planet, with the phosphorescent gleams of great cities showing here and there through gaps in the clouds. The disc of darkness had already blanked out a huge section of the Milky Way; in a few minutes, it would start to encroach upon the Sun.

The light was fading. A purple, twilight hue – the glow of many sunsets, thousands of miles below – was falling across the sail, as *Diana* slipped into the shadow of Earth. The Sun plummeted below that invisible horizon. Within minutes, it was night.

Merton looked back along the orbit he had traced now a quarter of the way around the world. One by one he saw the brilliant stars of the other yachts wink out, as they joined him in the brief night. It would be an hour before the Sun emerged from that enormous black shield, and through all that time they would be completely helpless, coasting without power.

He switched on the external spotlight and started to search the now darkened sail with its beam. Already, the thousands of acres of film were beginning to wrinkle and become flaccid; the shroud-lines were slackening, and must be wound in lest they become entangled. But all this was expected; everything was going as planned.

Forty miles astern, *Arachne* and *Santa Maria* were not so lucky. Merton learnt of their troubles when the radio burst into life on the emergency circuit.

'Number Two, Number Six – this is Control. You are on a collision course. Your orbits will intersect in sixty-five minutes! Do you require assistance?'

There was a long pause while the two skippers digested this bad news. Merton wondered who was to blame; perhaps one yacht had been trying to shadow the other, and had not completed the manoeuvre before they were both caught in darkness. Now there was nothing that either could do; they were slowly but inexorably converging, unable to change course by a fraction of a degree.'

Yet, sixty-five minutes! That would just bring them out into the sunlight again, as they emerged from the shadow of the Earth. They still had a slim chance, if their sails could snatch enough power to avoid a crash. There must be some frantic calculations going on, aboard *Arachne* and *Santa Maria.*

Arachne answered first; her reply was just what Merton had expected.

'Number Six calling Control. We don't need assistance, thank you. We'll work this out for ourselves.'

I wonder, thought Merton. But at least it will be interesting to watch. The first real drama of the race was approaching – exactly above the line of midnight on the sleeping Earth.

For the next hour, Merton's own sail kept him too busy to worry about *Arachne* and *Santa Maria*. It was hard to keep a good watch on that fifty million square feet of dim plastic out there in the darkness, illuminated only by his narrow spotlight and the rays of the still distant Moon. From now on, for almost half his orbit round the Earth, he must keep the whole of this immense area edge-on to the Sun. During the next twelve or fourteen hours, the sail would be a useless encumbrance; for he would be heading back into the Sun, and its rays could only drive him backwards along his orbit. It was a pity that he could not furl the sail completely, until he was ready to use it again. But no one had yet found a practical way of doing this.

Far below, there was the first hint of dawn along the edge of the Earth. In ten minutes, the Sun would emerge from its eclipse; the coasting yachts would come to life again as the blast of radiation struck their sails. That would be the moment of crisis for *Arachne* and *Santa Maria* – and indeed, for all of them.

Merton swung the periscope until he found the two dark shadows drifting against the stars. They were very close together – perhaps less than three miles apart. They might, he decided, just be able to make it ...

Dawn flashed like an explosion along the rim of Earth, as the Sun rose out of the Pacific. The sail and shroud-lines glowed a brief crimson, then gold, then blazed with the pure white light of day. The needles of the dynamometers began to lift from their zeros – but only just. *Diana* was still almost completely weightless, for with the sail pointing towards the Sun, her acceleration was now only a few millionths of a gravity.

But *Arachne* and *Santa Maria* were crowding on all the sail they could manage, in their desperate attempt to keep

131

apart. Now, while there was less than two miles between them, their glittering plastic clouds were unfurling and expanding with agonizing slowness, as they felt the first delicate push of the Sun's rays. Almost every TV screen on Earth would be mirroring this protracted drama; and even now, at this very last minute, it was impossible to tell what the outcome would be.

The two skippers were stubborn men. Either could have cut his sail, and fallen back to give the other a chance; but neither would do so. Too much prestige, too many millions, too many reputations, were at stake. And so, silently and softly as snowflakes falling on a winter night, *Arachne* and *Santa Maria* collided.

The square kite crawled almost imperceptibly into the circular spider's-web; the long ribbons of the shroud-lines twisted and tangled together with dreamlike slowness. Even aboard *Diana*, busy with his own rigging, Merton could scarcely tear his eye away from this silent, long drawn out disaster.

For more than ten minutes the billowing, shining clouds continued to merge into one inextricable mass. Then the crew capsules tore loose and went their separate ways, missing each other by hundreds of yards. With a flare of rockets, the safety launches hurried to pick them up.

That leaves five of us, thought Merton. He felt sorry for the skippers who had so thoroughly eliminated each other, only a few hours after the start of the race; but they were young men, and would have another chance.

Within minutes, the five had dropped to four. From the very beginning, Merton had had doubts about the slowly rotating *Sunbeam*. Now he saw them justified.

The Martian ship had failed to tack properly; her spin had given her too much stability. Her great ring of a sail was turning to face the Sun, instead of being edge-on to it. She was being blown back along her course at almost her maximum acceleration.

That was about the most maddening thing that could happen to a skipper – worse even than a collision, for he could blame only himself. But no one would feel much sympathy for the frustrated colonials, as they dwindled slowly astern. They had made too many brash boasts before the race, and what had happened to them was poetic justice.

Yet it would not do to write off *Sunbeam* completely. With almost half a million miles still to go, she might still pull ahead. Indeed, if there were a few more casualties, she might be the only one to complete the race. It had happened before.

However, the next twelve hours were uneventful, as the Earth waxed in the sky from new to full. There was little to do while the fleet drifted round the unpowered half of its orbit, but Merton did not find the time hanging heavily on his hands. He caught a few hours' sleep, ate two meals, wrote up his log, and became involved in several more radio interviews. Sometimes, though rarely, he talked to the other skippers, exchanging greetings and friendly taunts. But most of the time he was content to float in weightless relaxation, beyond all the cares of Earth, happier than he had been for many years. He was – as far as any man could be in space – master of his own fate, sailing the ship upon which he had lavished so much skill, so much love, that she had become part of his very being.

The next casualty came when they were passing the line between Earth and Sun, and were just beginning the powered half of the orbit. Aboard *Diana,* Merton saw the great sail stiffen as it tilted to catch the rays that drove it. The acceleration began to climb up from the microgravities, though it would be hours yet before it would reach its maximum value.

It would never reach it for *Gossamer*. The moment when power came on again was always critical, and she failed to

133

survive it.

Blair's radio commentary, which Merton had left running at low volume, alerted him with the news: 'Hullo, *Gossamer* has the wriggles!' He hurried to the periscope, but at first could see nothing wrong with the great circular disc of *Gossamer's* sail. It was difficult to study it, as it was almost edge-on to him and so appeared as a thin ellipse; but presently he saw that it was twisting back and forth in slow, irresistible oscillations. Unless the crew could damp out these waves, by properly timed but gentle tugs on the shroud-lines, the sail would tear itself to pieces.

They did their best, and after twenty minutes it seemed that they had succeeded. Then, somewhere near the centre of the sail, the plastic film began to rip. It was slowly driven outwards by the radiation pressure, like smoke coiling upwards from a fire. Within a quarter of an hour, nothing was left but the delicate tracery of the radial spars that had supported the great web. Once again there was a flare of rockets, as a launch moved in to retrieve the *Gossamer's* capsule and her dejected crew.

'Getting rather lonely up here, isn't it?' said a conversational voice over the ship-to-ship radio.

'Not for you, Dimitri,' retorted Merton. 'You've still got company back there at the end of the field. I'm the one who's lonely, up here in front.' It was not an idle boast. By this time *Diana* was three hundred miles ahead of the next competitor, and his lead should increase still more rapidly in the hours to come.

Aboard *Lebedev*, Dimitri Markoff gave a good-natured chuckle. He did not sound, Merton thought, at all like a man who had resigned himself to defeat.

'Remember the legend of the tortoise and the hare,' answered the Russian. 'A lot can happen in the next quarter-million miles.'

It happened much sooner than that, when they had completed their first orbit of Earth and were passing the starting line again – though thousands of miles higher, thanks to the extra energy the Sun's rays had given them. Merton had taken careful sights on the other yachts, and had fed the figures into the computer. The answer it gave for *Woomera* was so absurd that he immediately did a recheck.

There was no doubt of it – the Australasians were catching up at a fantastic rate. No solar yacht could possibly have such an acceleration, unless —

A swift look through the periscope gave the answer. *Woomera's* rigging, pared back to the very minimum of mass, had given way. It was her sail alone, still maintaining its shape, that was racing up behind him like a handkerchief blown before the wind. Two hours later it fluttered past, less than twenty miles away. But long before that, the Australasians had joined the growing crowd aboard the Commodore's launch.

So now it was a straight fight between *Diana* and *Lebedev* – for though the Martians had not given up, they were a thousand miles astern and no longer counted as a serious threat. For that matter, it was hard to see what *Lebedev* could do to overtake *Diana's* lead. But all the way round the second lap – through eclipse again, and the long, slow drift against the Sun, Merton felt a growing unease.

He knew the Russian pilots and designers. They had been trying to win this race for twenty years and after all, it was only fair that they should, for had not Pyotr Nikolayevich Lebedev been the first man to detect the pressure of sunlight, back at the very beginning of the Twentieth Century? But they had never succeeded.

And they would never stop trying. Dimitri was up to something – and it would be spectacular.

Aboard the official launch, a thousand miles behind the racing yachts, Commodore van Stratten looked at the radiogram with angry dismay. It had travelled more than a hundred million miles, from the chain of solar observatories swinging high above the blazing surface of the Sun, and it brought the worst possible news.

The Commodore – his title, of course, was purely honorary – back on Earth he was Professor of Astrophysics at Harvard – had been half expecting it. Never before had the race been arranged so late in the season; there had been many delays, they had gambled and now, it seemed they might all lose.

Deep beneath the surface of the Sun, enormous forces were gathering. At any moment, the energies of a million hydrogen bombs might burst forth in the awesome explosion known as a solar flare. Climbing at millions of miles an hour, an invisible fireball many times the size of Earth would leap from the Sun, and head out across space.

The cloud of electrified gas would probably miss the Earth completely. But if it did not, it would arrive in just over a day. Spaceships could protect themselves, with their shielding and their powerful magnetic screen. But the lightly-built solar yachts, with their paper-thin walls, were defenceless against such a menace. The crews would have to be taken off, and the race abandoned.

John Merton still knew nothing of this as he brought *Diana* round the Earth for the second time. If all went well, this would be the last circuit, both for him and the Russians. They had spiralled upwards by thousands of miles, gaining energy from the Sun's rays. On this lap, they should escape from Earth completely – and head outwards on the long run to the Moon. It was a straight race now. *Sunbeam's* crew had finally withdrawn, exhausted, after battling valiantly with their spinning sail for more than a hundred thousand miles.

Merton did not feel tired; he had eaten and slept well, and *Diana* was behaving herself admirably. The autopilot, tensioning the rigging like a busy little spider, kept the great sail trimmed to the Sun more accurately than any human skipper. Though by this time, the two square miles of plastic sheet must have been riddled by hundreds of micrometeorites, the pinhead-sized punctures had produced no falling off to thrust.

He had only two worries. The first was shroud-line Number Eight, which could no longer be adjusted properly. Without any warning, the reel had jammed; even after all these years of astronautical engineering, bearings sometimes seized up in vacuum. He could neither lengthen nor shorten the line, and would have to navigate as best he could with the others. Luckily, the most difficult manoeuvres were over. From now on, *Diana* would have the Sun behind her as she sailed straight down the solar wind. And as the old-time sailors often said, it was easy to handle a boat when the wind was blowing over your shoulder.

His other worry was *Lebedev*, still dogging his heels three hundred miles astern. The Russian yacht had shown remarkable manoeuvrability, thanks to the four great panels that could be tilted around the central sail. All her flip-overs as she rounded Earth had been carried out with superb precision; but to gain manoeuvrability she must have sacrificed speed. You could not have it both ways. In the long, straight haul ahead, Merton should be able to hold his own. Yet he could not be certain of victory until, three or four days from now, *Diana* went flashing past the far side of the Moon.

And then, in the fiftieth hour of the race, near the end of the second orbit around Earth, Markoff sprang his little surprise.

'Hello, John,' he said casually, over the ship-to-ship circuit. 'I'd like you to watch this. It should be interesting.'

Merton drew himself across to the periscope and turned up the magnification to the limit. There in the field of view, a most improbable sight against the background of the stars, was the glittering Maltese cross of *Lebedev*, very small but very clear. And then, as he watched, the four arms of the cross slowly detached themselves from the central square and went drifting away, with all their spars and rigging, into space.

Markoff had jettisoned all unnecessary mass, now that he was coming up to escape velocity and need no longer plod patiently around the Earth, gaining momentum on each circuit. From now on, *Lebedev* would be almost unsteerable – but that did not matter. All the tricky navigation lay behind her. It was as if an old-time yachtsman had deliberately thrown away his rudder and heavy keel – knowing that the rest of the race would be straight downwind over a calm sea.

'Congratulations, Dimitri,' Merton radioed. 'It's a neat trick. But it's not good enough – you can't catch up now.'

'I've not finished yet,' the Russian answered. 'There's an old winter's tale in my country, about a sleigh being chased by wolves. To save himself, the driver has to throw off the passengers one by one. Do you see the analogy?'

Merton did, all too well. On this final straight lap, Dimitri no longer needed his co-pilot. *Lebedev* could really be stripped down for action.

'Alexis won't be very happy about this,' Merton replied. 'Besides, it's against the rules.'

'Alexis isn't happy, but I'm the captain. He'll just have to wait around for ten minutes until the Commodore picks him up. And the regulations say nothing about the size of the crew – you should know that.'

Merton did not answer. He was too busy doing some hurried calculations, based on what he knew of *Lebedev's* design. By the time he had finished, he knew that the race was still in doubt. *Lebedev* would be catching up with him at just about the time he hoped to pass the Moon.

But the outcome of the race was already being decided, ninety-two million miles away.

On Solar Observatory Three, far inside the orbit of Mercury, the automatic instruments recorded the whole history of the flare. A hundred million square miles of the Sun's surface suddenly exploded in such blue-white fury that, by comparison, the rest of the disc paled to a dull glow. Out of that seething inferno, twisting and turning like a living creature in the magnetic fields of its own creation, soared the electrified plasma of the great flare. Ahead of it, moving at the speed of light, went the warning flash of ultra-violet and X-rays. That would reach Earth in eight minutes, and was relatively harmless. Not so the charged atoms that were following behind at their leisurely four million miles an hour – and which, in just over a day, would engulf *Diana*, *Lebedev*, and their accompanying little fleet in a cloud of lethal radiation.

The Commodore left his decision to the last possible minute. Even when the jet of plasma had been tracked past the orbit of Venus, there was a chance that it might miss the Earth. But when it was less than four hours away, and had already been picked up by the Moon-based radar network, he knew that there was no hope. All solar sailing was over for the next five or six years until the Sun was quiet again.

A great sigh of disappointment swept across the Solar System. *Diana* and *Lebedev* were halfway between Earth and Moon, running neck and neck – and now no one would ever know which was the better boat. The enthusiasts would argue the result for years; history would merely record: Race cancelled owing to solar storm.

When John Merton received the order, he felt a bitterness he had not known since childhood. Across the years, sharp and clear, came the memory of his tenth birthday. He had been promised an exact scale model of the famous spaceship *Morning Star*, and for weeks had been planning how he would assemble it, where he would hang it up in his bedroom. And then, at the last moment, his father had broken the news. 'I'm sorry, John – it costs too much money. Maybe next year ...'

Half a century and a successful lifetime later, he was a heartbroken boy again.

For a moment, he thought of disobeying the Commodore. Suppose he sailed on, ignoring the warning? Even if the race were abandoned, he could make a crossing to the Moon that would stand in the record books for generations.

But that would be worse than stupidity. It would be suicide – and a very unpleasant form of suicide. He had seen men die of radiation poisoning, when the magnetic shielding of their ships had failed in deep space. No – nothing was worth that ...

He felt as sorry for Dimitri Markoff as for himself; they both deserved to win, and now victory would go to neither. No man could argue with the Sun in one of its rages, even though he might ride upon its beams to the edge of space.

Only fifty miles astern now, the Commodore's launch was drawing alongside *Lebedev*, preparing to take off her skipper. There went the silver sail, as Dimitri – with feelings that he would share – cut the rigging. The tiny capsule would be taken back to earth, perhaps to be used again – but a sail was spread for one voyage only.

He could press the jettison button now, and save his rescuers a few minutes of time. But he would not do so. He wanted to stay aboard to the very end, on the little boat that had been for so long a part of his dreams and his life. The great sail was spread now at right angles to the Sun, exerting its utmost thrust. Long ago it had torn him clear of Earth – and *Diana* was still gaining speed.

Then, out of nowhere, beyond all doubt or hesitation, he knew what must be done. For the last time, he sat down

140

before the computer that had navigated him halfway to the Moon.

When he had finished, he packed the log and his few personal belongings. Clumsily – for he was out of practice, and it was not an easy job to do by oneself – he climbed into the emergency survival suit.

He was just sealing the helmet when the Commodore's voice called over the radio. 'We'll be alongside in five minutes, Captain. Please cut your sail so we won't foul it.'

John Merton, first and last skipper of the sun-yacht *Diana*, hesitated for a moment. He looked for the last time round the tiny cabin, with its shining instruments and its neatly arranged controls, now all locked in their final positions. Then he said to the microphone: 'I'm abandoning ship. Take your time to pick me up. *Diana* can look after herself.'

There was no reply from the Commodore, and for that he was grateful. Professor van Stratten would have guessed what was happening – and would know that, in these final moments, he wished to be left alone.

He did not bother to exhaust the airlock, and the rush of escaping gas blew him gently out into space; the thrust he gave her then was his last gift to *Diana*. She dwindled away from him, sail glittering splendidly in the sunlight that would be hers for centuries to come. Two days from now she would flash past the Moon; but the Moon, like the Earth, could never catch her. Without his mass to slow her down, she would gain two thousand miles an hour in every day of sailing. In a month, she would be travelling faster than any ship that man had ever built.

As the Sun's rays weakened with distance, so her acceleration would fall. But even at the orbit of Mars, she would be gaining a thousand miles an hour in every day. Long before then, she would be moving too swiftly for the Sun itself to hold her. Faster than any comet that had ever streaked in from the stars, she would be heading out into the abyss.

The glare of rockets, only a few miles away, caught Merton's eye. The launch was approaching to pick him up at thousands of times the acceleration that *Diana* could ever attain. But engines could burn for a few minutes only, before they exhausted their fuel – while *Diana* would still be gaining speed, driven outwards by the Sun's eternal fires, for ages yet to come.

'Good-bye, little ship,' said John Merton. 'I wonder what eyes will see you next, how many thousand years from now?'

At last he felt at peace, as the blunt torpedo of the launch nosed up beside him. He would never win the race to the Moon; but his would be the first of all man's ships to set sail on the long journey to the stars.

A MEETING WITH MEDUSA

1. A DAY TO REMEMBER

THE *Queen Elizabeth* was over three miles above the Grand Canyon, dawdling along at a comfortable hundred and eighty, when Howard Falcon spotted the camera platform closing in from the right. He had been expecting it – nothing else was cleared to fly at this altitude – but he was not too happy to have company. Although he welcomed any signs of public interest, he also wanted as much empty sky as he could get. After all, he was the first man in history to navigate a ship three-tenths of a mile long ...

So far, this first test flight had gone perfectly; ironically enough, the only problem had been the century-old aircraft carrier *Chairman Mao*, borrowed from the San Diego Naval Museum for support operations. Only one of *Mao*'s four nuclear reactors was still operating, and the old battle-wagon's top speed was barely thirty knots. Luckily, the wind speed at sea level had been less than half this, so it had not been too difficult to maintain still air on the flight deck. Though there had been a few anxious moments during gusts, when the mooring lines had been dropped, the great dirigible had risen smoothly, straight up into the sky, as if on an invisible elevator. If all went well, *Queen Elizabeth IV* would not meet *Chairman Mao* again for another week.

Everything was under control; all test instruments gave normal readings. Commander Falcon decided to go upstairs and watch the rendezvous. He handed over to his second officer, and walked out into the transparent tubeway that led through the heart of the ship. There, as always, he was

143

overwhelmed by the spectacle of the largest single space ever enclosed by man.

The ten spherical gas cells, each more than a hundred feet across, were ranged one behind the other like a line of gigantic soap bubbles. The tough plastic was so clear that he could see through the whole length of the array, and make out details of the elevator mechanism, more than a third of a mile from his vantage point. All around him, like a three-dimensional maze, was the structural framework of the ship – the great longitudinal girders running from nose to tail, the fifteen hoops that were the circular ribs of this sky-borne colossus, and whose varying sizes defined its graceful, streamlined profile.

At this low speed, there was little sound – merely the soft rush of wind over the envelope and an occasional creak of metal as the pattern of stresses changed. The shadowless light from the rows of lamps far overhead gave the whole scene a curiously submarine quality, and to Falcon this was enhanced by the spectacle of the translucent gasbags. He had once encountered a squadron of large but harmless jellyfish, pulsing their mindless way above a shallow tropical reef, and the plastic bubbles that gave *Queen Elizabeth* her lift often reminded him of these – especially when changing pressures made them crinkle and scatter new patterns of reflected light.

He walked down the axis of the ship until he came to the forward elevator, between gas cells one and two. Riding up to the Observation Deck, he noticed that it was uncomfortably hot, and dictated a brief memo to himself on his pocket recorder. The *Queen* obtained almost a quarter of her buoyancy from the unlimited amounts of waste heat produced by her fusion power plant. On this lightly loaded flight, indeed, only six of the ten gas cells contained helium; the remaining four were full of air. Yet she still carried two hundred tons of water as ballast. However, running the cells at high temperatures did produce problems in refrigerating the access ways; it was obvious that a little more work would have to be done there.

A refreshing blast of cooler air hit him in the face when he stepped out on to the Observation Deck and into the dazzling sunlight streaming through the plexiglass roof. Half a dozen workmen, with an equal number of super-chimp assistants, were busily laying the partly completed dance floor, while others were installing electric wiring and fixing furniture. It was a scene of controlled chaos, and Falcon found it hard to believe that everything would be ready for the maiden voyage, only four weeks ahead. Well, that was not *his* problem, thank goodness. He was merely the Captain, not the Cruise Director.

The human workers waved to him, and the 'simps' flashed toothy smiles, as he walked through the confusion, into the already completed Skylounge. This was his favourite place in the whole ship, and he knew that once she was operating he would never again have it all to himself. He would allow himself just five minutes of private enjoyment.

He called the bridge, checked that everything was still in order, and relaxed into one of the comfortable swivel chairs. Below, in a curve that delighted the eye, was the unbroken silver sweep of the ship's envelope. He was perched at the highest point, surveying the whole immensity of the largest vehicle ever built. And when he had tired of that – all the way out to the horizon was the fantastic wilderness carved by the Colorado River in half a billion years of time.

Apart from the camera platform (it had now fallen back and was filming from amidships), he had the sky to himself. It was blue and empty, clear down to the horizon. In his grandfather's day, Falcon knew, it would have been streaked with vapour trails and stained with smoke. Both had gone: the aerial garbage had vanished with the primitive technologies that spawned it, and the long-distance transportation of this age arced too far beyond the strato-sphere for any sight or sound of it to reach Earth. Once again, the lower atmosphere belonged to the birds and the clouds – and now to *Queen Elizabeth IV*.

It was true, as the old pioneers had said at the beginning of the twentieth century: this was the only way to travel – in silence and luxury, breathing the air around you and not cut off from it, near enough to the surface to watch the ever-changing beauty of land and sea. The subsonic jets of the 1980s, packed with hundreds of passengers seated ten abreast, could not even begin to match such comfort and spaciousness.

Of course, the Queen would never be an economic propo-sition, and even if her projected sister ships were built, only a few of the world's quarter of a billion inhabitants would ever enjoy this silent gliding through the sky. But a secure and prosperous global society could afford such follies and indeed needed them for their novelty and entertainment. There were at least a million men on Earth whose dis-cretionary income exceeded a thousand new dollars a year, so the *Queen* would not lack for passengers.

Falcon's pocket communicator beeped. The co-pilot was calling from the bridge.

'O.K. for rendezvous, Captain? We've got all the data we need from this run, and the TV people are getting im-patient.'

Falcon glanced at the camera platform, now matching his speed a tenth of a mile away.

'O.K.,' he replied. 'Proceed as arranged. I'll watch from here.'

He walked back through the busy chaos of the Observa-tion Deck so that he could have a better view amidships. As he did so, he could feel the change of vibration underfoot; by the time he had reached the rear of the lounge, the ship had come to rest. Using his master key, he let himself out on to the small external platform flaring from the end of the deck; half a dozen people could stand here, with only low guardrails separating them from the vast sweep of the envelope – and from the ground, thousands of feet below. It was an exciting place to be, and perfectly safe even when the ship was travelling at speed, for it was in the dead air behind the huge dorsal blister of the Observation Deck. Nevertheless, it was not intended that the passengers would have access to it; the view was a little too vertiginous.

The covers of the forward cargo hatch had already opened like giant trap doors, and the camera platform was hovering above them, preparing to descend. Along this route, in the years to come, would travel thousands of passengers and tons of supplies. Only on rare occasions would the *Queen* drop down to sea level and dock with her floating base.

A sudden gust of cross-wind slapped Falcon's cheek, and he tightened his grip on the guardrail. The Grand Canyon was a bad place for turbulence, though he did not expect much at this altitude. Without any real anxiety, he focused his attention on the descending platform, now about a hundred and fifty feet above the ship. He knew that the highly skilled operator who was flying the remotely controlled vehicle had performed this simple manoeuvre a dozen times already; it was inconceivable that he would have any difficulties.

Yet he seemed to be reacting rather sluggishly. That last gust had drifted the platform almost to the edge of the open hatchway. Surely the pilot could have corrected before this. . . . Did he have a control problem? It was very unlikely; these remotes had multiple-redundancy, fail-safe takeovers and any number of backup systems. Accidents were almost unheard of.

But there he went again, off to the left. Could the pilot be *drunk*? Improbable though that seemed, Falcon considered it seriously for a moment. Then he reached for his micro-

147

phone switch.

Once again, without warning, he was slapped violently in the face. He hardly felt it, for he was staring in horror at the camera platform. The distant operator was fighting for control, trying to balance the craft on its jets – but he was only making matters worse. The oscillations increased – twenty degrees, forty, sixty, ninety . . .

'Switch to automatic, you fool!' Falcon shouted uselessly into his microphone. 'Your manual control's not working!'

The platform flipped over on its back. The jets no longer supported it, but drove it swiftly downward. They had suddenly become allies of the gravity they had fought until this moment.

Falcon never heard the crash, though he felt it; he was already inside the Observation Deck, racing for the elevator that would take him down to the bridge. Workman shouted at him anxiously, asking what had happened. It would be many months before he knew the answer to that question.

Just as he was stepping into the elevator cage, he changed his mind. What if there was a power failure? Better be on the safe side, even if it took longer and time was the essence. He began to run down the spiral stairway enclosing the shaft.

Halfway down he paused for a second to inspect the damage. That damned platform had gone clear through the ship, rupturing two of the gas cells as it did so. They were still collapsing slowly, in great falling veils of plastic. He was not worried about the loss of lift – the ballast could easily take care of that, as long as eight cells remained intact. Far more serious was the possibility of structural damage. Already he could hear the great latticework around him groaning and protesting under its abnormal loads. It was not enough to have sufficient lift; unless it was properly distributed, the ship would break her back.

He was just resuming his descent when a superchimp,

shrieking with fright, came racing down the elevator shaft, moving with incredible speed, hand over hand, along the *outside* of the latticework. In its terror, the poor beast had torn off its company uniform, perhaps in an unconscious attempt to regain the freedom of its ancestors.

Falcon, still descending as swiftly as he could, watched its approach with some alarm. A distraught simp was a powerful and potentially dangerous animal, especially if fear overcame its conditioning. As it overtook him, it started to call out a string of words, but they were all jumbled together, and the only one he could recognize was a plaintive, frequently repeated 'boss'. Even now, Falcon realized, it looked towards humans for guidance. He felt sorry for the creature, involved in a man-made disaster beyond its comprehension, and for which it bore no responsibility.

It stopped opposite him, on the other side of the lattice; there was nothing to prevent it from coming through the open framework if it wished. Now its face was only inches from his, and he was looking straight into the terrified eyes. Never before had he been so close to a simp, and able to study its features in such detail. He felt that strange mingling of kinship and discomfort that all men experience when they gave thus into the mirror of time.

His presence seemed to have calmed the creature. Falcon pointed up the shaft, back towards the Observation Deck, and said very clearly and precisely: 'Boss – boss – *go*.' To his relief, the simp understood; it gave him a grimace that might have been a smile, and at once started to race back the way it had come. Falcon had given it the best advice he could. If any safety remained aboard the *Queen*, it was in that direction. But his duty lay in the other.

He had almost completed his descent when, with a sound of rending metal, the vessel pitched nose down, and the lights went out. But he could still see quite well, for a shaft of sunlight streamed through the open hatch and the huge tear in the envelope. Many years ago he had stood in a great cathedral nave watching the light pouring through the stained-glass windows and forming pools of multicoloured radiance on the ancient flagstones. The dazzling shaft of sunlight through the ruined fabric high above reminded him of that moment. He was in a cathedral of metal, falling down the sky.

When he reached the bridge, and was able for the first time to look outside, he was horrified to see how close the ship was to the ground. Only three thousand feet below were the beautiful and deadly pinnacles of rock and the red rivers of mud that were still carving their way down into the past. There was no level area anywhere in sight where a ship as large as the *Queen* could come to rest on an even keel.

A glance at the display board told him that all the ballast had gone. However, rate of descent had been reduced to a few yards a second; they still had a fighting chance.

Without a word, Falcon eased himself into the pilot's seat and took over such control as still remained. The instrument board showed him everything he wished to know; speech was superfluous. In the background, he could hear the Communications Officer giving a running report over the radio. By this time, all the news channels of Earth would have been pre-empted, and he could imagine the utter frustration of the programme controllers. One of the most spectacular wrecks in history was occurring – without a single camera to record it. The last moments of the *Queen* would never fill millions with awe and terror, as had those of the *Hindenburg*, a century and a half before.

Now the ground was only about seventeen hundred feet away, still coming up slowly. Though he had full thrust, he had not dared to use it, lest the weakened structure collapse; but now he realized that he had no choice. The wind was taking them towards a fork in the canyon, where the river was split by a wedge of rock like the prow of some gigantic, fossilized ship of stone. If she continued on her present course, the *Queen* would straddle that triangular plateau and come to rest with at least a third of her length jutting out over nothingness; she would snap like a rotten stick.

Far away, above the sound of straining metal and escaping gas, came the familiar whistle of the jets as Falcon opened up the lateral thrusters. The ship staggered, and began to slew to port. The shriek of tearing metal was now almost continuous – and the rate of descent had started to increase ominously. A glance at the damage-control board showed that cell number five had just gone.

The ground was only yards away. Even now, he could not tell whether his manoeuvre would succeed or fail. He switched the thrust vectors over to vertical, giving maximum life to reduce the force of impact.

The crash seemed to last forever. It was not violent – merely prolonged, and irresistible. It seemed that the whole universe was falling about them.

The sound of crunching metal came nearer, as if some great beast were eating its way through the dying ship.

Then floor and ceiling closed upon him like a vice.

2. 'BECAUSE IT'S THERE'

'Why do you want to go to Jupiter?'

'As Springer said when he lifted for Pluto – "because it's there".'

'Thanks. Now we've got *that* out of the way – the real reason.'

Howard Falcon smiled, though only those who knew him well could have interpreted the slight, leathery grimace. Webster was one of them; for more than twenty years they had been involved in each other's projects. They had shared triumphs and disasters – including the greatest disaster of all.

'Well, Springer's cliché is still valid. We've landed on all the terrestrial planets, but none of the gas giants. They are the only real challenge left in the solar system.'

'An expensive one. Have you worked out the cost?'

'As well as I can; here are the estimates. Remember, though – this isn't a one-shot mission, but a transportation system. Once it's proved out, it can be used over and over again. And it will open up not merely Jupiter, but *all* the giants.'

Webster looked at the figures, and whistled.

'Why not start with an easier planet – Uranus, for example? Half the gravity, and less than half the escape velocity. Quieter weather, too – if that's the right word for it.'

Webster had certainly done his homework. But that, of course, was why he was head of Long-Range Planning.

'There's very little saving – when you allow for the extra distance and the logistics problems. For Jupiter, we can use the facilities of Ganymede. Beyond Saturn, we'd have to establish a new supply base.'

Logical, thought Webster; but he was sure that it was not the important reason. Jupiter was lord of the solar system; Falcon would be interested in no lesser challenge.

'Besides,' Falcon continued, 'Jupiter is a major scientific scandal. It's more than a hundred years since its radio storms were discovered, but we still don't know what causes them – and the Great Red Spot is as big a mystery as ever. That's why I can get matching funds from the Bureau of Astronautics. Do you know how many probes they have dropped into that atmosphere?'

'A couple of hundred, I believe.'

'*Three* hundred and twenty-six, over the last fifty years – about a quarter of them total failures. Of course, they've learned a hell of a lot, but they've barely scratched the planet. Do you realize how *big* it is?'

'More than ten times the size of Earth.'

'Yes, yes – but do you know what that really means?'

Falcon pointed to the large globe in the corner of Webster's office.

'Look at India – how small it seems. Well, if you skinned Earth and spread it out on the surface of Jupiter, it would look about as big as India does here.'

There was a long silence while Webster contemplated the equation: Jupiter is to Earth as Earth is to India. Falcon had – deliberately, of course – chosen the best possible example ...

Was it already ten years ago? Yes, it must have been. The crash lay seven years in the past (that date was engraved on his heart), and those initial tests had taken place three years before the first and last flight of the *Queen Elizabeth*.

Ten years ago, then, Commander (no, Lieutenant) Falcon had invited him to a preview – a three-day drift across the northern plains of India, within sight of the Himalayas. 'Perfectly safe,' he had promised. 'It will get you away from the office – and will teach you what this whole thing is about.'

Webster had not been disappointed. Next to his first journey to the Moon, it had been the most memorable experience of his life. And yet, as Falcon had assured him, it had been perfectly safe, and quite uneventful.

They had taken off from Srinagar just before dawn, with the huge silver bubble of the balloon already catching the first light of the Sun. The ascent had been made in total silence; there was none of the roaring propane burners that had lifted the hot-air balloons of an earlier age. All the heat they needed came from the little pulsed-fusion reactor, weighing only about two hundred and twenty pounds, hanging in the open mouth of the envelope. While they were climbing, its laser was zapping ten times a second, igniting the merest whiff of deuterium fuel. Once they reached altitude, it would fire only a few times a minute, making up for the heat lost through the great gasbag overhead.

And so, even while they were almost a mile above the ground, they could hear dogs barking, people shouting, bells ringing. Slowly the vast, Sun-smitten landscape expanded around them. Two hours later, they had levelled out at three miles and were taking frequent draughts of oxygen. They could relax and admire the scenery; the on-board instrumentation was doing all the work – gathering the information that would be required by the designers of the still-unnamed liner of the skies.

It was a perfect day. The southwest monsoon would not break for another month, and there was hardly a cloud in the sky. Time seemed to have come to a stop; they resented the hourly radio reports which interrupted their reverie. And all around, to the horizon and far beyond, was that infinite, ancient landscape, drenched with history – a patchwork of villages, fields, temples, lakes, irrigation canals . . .

With a real effort, Webster broke the hypnotic spell of that ten-year-old memory. It had converted him to lighter-than-air flight – and it had made him realize the enormous size of India, even in a world that could be circled within ninety minutes. And yet, he repeated to himself, Jupiter is to Earth as Earth is to India . . .

'Granted your argument,' he said, 'and supposing the funds are available, there's another question you have to answer. Why should you do better than the – what is it – three hundred and twenty-six robot probes that have already made the trip?'

'I am better qualified than they were – as an observer, and as a pilot. *Especially* as a pilot. Don't forget – I've more experience of lighter-than-air flight than anyone in the world.'

'You could still serve as controller, and sit safely on Ganymede.'

'*But that's just the point!* They've already done that. Don't you remember what killed the *Queen*?'

Webster knew perfectly well; but he merely answered: 'Go on.'

'*Time lag – time lag*! That idiot of a platform controller thought he was using a local radio circuit. But he'd been accidentally switched through a satellite – oh, maybe it wasn't his fault, but he should have noticed. That's a half-second time lag for the round trip. Even then it wouldn't have mattered flying in calm air. It was the turbulence over the Grand Canyon that did it. When the platform tipped, and he corrected for that – it had already tipped the other way. Ever tried to drive a car over a bumpy road with a half-second delay in the steering?'

'No, and I don't intend to try. But I can imagine it.'

'Well, Ganymede is a million kilometres from Jupiter. That means a round-trip delay of six seconds. No, you need a controller on the spot – to handle emergencies in real time. Let me show you something. Mind if I use this?'

'Go ahead.'

Falcon picked up a postcard that was lying on Webster's desk; they were almost obsolete on Earth, but this one showed a 3-D view of a Martian landscape, and was decorated with exotic and expensive stamps. He held it so that it dangled vertically.

'This is an old trick, but helps to make my point. Place your thumb and finger on either side, not quite touching. That's right.'

Webster put out his hand, almost but not quite gripping the card.

'Now catch it.'

Falcon waited for a few seconds; then, without warning, he let go of the card. Webster's thumb and finger closed on empty air.

'I'll do it again, just to show there's no deception. You see?'

Once again, the falling card had slipped through Webster's fingers.

'Now you try it on me.'

This time, Webster grasped the card and dropped it without warning. It had scarcely moved before Falcon had caught it. Webster almost imagined he could hear a click, so swift was the other's reaction.

'When they put me together again,' Falcon remarked in an expressionless voice, 'the surgeons made some improvements. This is one of them – and there are others. I want to make the most of them. Jupiter is the place where I can do it.'

Webster stared for long seconds at the fallen card, absorbing the improbable colours of the Trivium Charontis Escarpment. Then he said quietly: 'I understand. How long do you think it will take?'

'With your help, plus the Bureau, plus all the science foundations we can drag in – oh, three years. Then a year for trials – we'll have to send in at least two test models. So, with luck – five years.'

'That's about what I thought. I hope you get your luck; you've earned it. But there's one thing I won't do.'

'What's that?'

'Next time you go ballooning, don't expect *me* as passenger.'

3. THE WORLD OF THE GODS

The fall from Jupiter V to Jupiter itself takes only three and a half hours. Few men could have slept on so awesome a journey. Sleep was a weakness that Howard Falcon hated,

156

and the little he still required brought dreams that time had not yet been able to exorcize. But he could expect no rest in the three days that lay ahead, and must seize what he could during the long fall down into that ocean of clouds, some sixty thousand miles below.

As soon as *Kon-Tiki* had entered her transfer orbit and all the computer checks were satisfactory, he prepared for the last sleep he might ever know. It seemed appropriate that at almost the same moment Jupiter eclipsed the bright and tiny Sun as he swept into the monstrous shadow of the planet. For a few minutes a strange golden twilight enveloped the ship; then a quarter of the sky became an utterly black hole in space, while the rest was a blaze of stars. No matter how far one travelled across the solar system, *they* never changed; these same constellations now shone on Earth, millions of miles away. The only novelties here were the small, pale crescents of Callisto and Ganymede; doubtless there were a dozen other moons up there in the sky, but they were all much too tiny, and too distant, for the unaided eye to pick them out.

'Closing down for two hours,' he reported to the mother ship, hanging almost a thousand miles above the desolate rocks of Jupiter V, in the radiation shadow of the tiny satellite. If it never served any other useful purpose, Jupiter V was a cosmic bulldozer perpetually sweeping up the charged particles that made it unhealthy to linger close to Jupiter. Its wake was almost free of radiation, and there a ship could park in perfect safety, while death sleeted invisibly all around.

Falcon switched on the sleep inducer, and consciousness faded swiftly out as the electric pulses surged gently through his brain. While *Kon-Tiki* fell towards Jupiter, gaining speed second by second in that enormous gravitational field, he slept without dreams. They always came when he awoke; and he had brought his nightmares with him from Earth.

Yet he never dreamed of the crash itself, though he often found himself again face to face with that terrified super-chimp, as he descended the spiral stairway between the collapsing gasbags. None of the simps had survived; those that were not killed outright were so badly injured that they had been painlessly 'euthed'. He sometimes wondered why he dreamed only of this doomed creature – which he had never met before the last minutes of its life – and not of the friends and colleagues he had lost aboard the dying *Queen*.

The dreams he feared most always began with his first return to consciousness. There had been little physical pain; in fact, there had been no sensation of any kind. He was in darkness and silence, and did not even seem to be breathing. And – strangest of all – he could not locate his limbs. He could move neither his hands nor his feet, because he did not know where they were.

The silence had been the first to yield. After hours, or days, he had become aware of a faint throbbing, and eventually, after long thought, he deduced that this was the beating of his own heart. That was the first of his many mistakes.

Then there had been faint pinpricks, sparkles of light, ghosts of pressures upon still-unresponsive limbs. One by one his senses had returned, and pain had come with them. He had had to learn everything anew, recapitulating infancy and babyhood. Though his memory was unaffected, and he could understand words that were spoken to him, it was months before he was able to answer except by the flicker of an eyelid. He could remember the moments of triumph when he had spoken the first word, turned the page of a book – and, finally, learned to move under his own power. *That* was a victory indeed, and it had taken him almost two years to prepare for it. A hundred times he had envied that dead superchimp, but *he* had been given no choice. The doctors had made their decision – and now, twelve years later, he was where no human being had ever travelled before, and moving faster than any man in history.

Kon-Tiki was just emerging from shadow, and the Jovian dawn bridged the sky ahead in a titanic bow of light, when the persistent buzz of the alarm dragged Falcon up from sleep. The inevitable nightmares (he had been trying to summon a nurse, but did not even have the strength to push the button) swiftly faded from consciousness. The greatest – and perhaps last – adventure of his life was before him.

He called Mission Control, now almost sixty thousand miles away and falling swiftly below the curve of Jupiter, to report that everything was in order. His velocity had just passed thirty-one miles a second (*that* was one for the books) and in half an hour *Kon-Tiki* would hit the outer fringes of the atmosphere, as he started on the most difficult re-entry in the entire solar system. Although scores of probes had survived this flaming ordeal, they had been tough, solidly packed masses of instrumentation, able to withstand several hundred gravities of drag. *Kon-Tiki* would hit peaks of thirty g's, and would average more than ten, before she came to rest in the upper reaches of the Jovian atmosphere. Very carefully and thoroughly, Falcon began to attach the elaborate system of restraints that would anchor him to the walls of the cabin. When he had finished, he was virtually a part of the ship's structure.

The clock was counting backward; one hundred seconds to re-entry. For better or worse, he was committed. In a minute and a half, he would graze the Jovian atmosphere, and would be caught irrevocably in the grip of the giant.

The countdown was three seconds late – not at all bad, considering the unknowns involved. From beyond the walls of the capsule came a ghostly sighing, which rose steadily to a high-pitched, screaming roar. The noise was quite different from that of a re-entry on Earth or Mars; in this thin atmosphere of hydrogen and helium, all sounds were transformed a couple of octaves upward. On Jupiter, even thunder would have falsetto overtones.

With the rising scream came mounting weight; within seconds, he was completely immobilized. His field of vision contracted until it embraced only the clock and the accelerometer; fifteen g, and four hundred and eighty seconds to go ...

He never lost consciousness; but then, he had not expected to. *Kon-Tiki*'s trail through the Jovian atmosphere must be really spectacular – by this time, thousands of miles long. Five hundred seconds after entry, the drag began to taper off: ten g, five g, two ... Then weight vanished almost completely. He was falling free, all his enormous orbital velocity destroyed.

There was a sudden jolt as the incandescent remnants of the heat shield were jettisoned. It had done its work and would not be needed again; Jupiter could have it now. He released all but two of the restraining buckles, and waited for the automatic sequencer to start the next, and most critical, series of events.

He did not see the first drogue parachute pop out, but he could feel the slight jerk, and the rate of fall diminished immediately. *Kon-Tiki* had lost all her horizontal speed and was going straight down at almost a thousand miles an hour. Everything depended on what happened in the next sixty seconds.

There went the second drogue. He looked up through the overhead window and saw, to his immense relief, that clouds of glittering foil were billowing out behind the falling ship. Like a great flower unfurling, the thousands of cubic yards of the balloon spread out across the sky, scooping up the thin gas until it was fully inflated. *Kon-Tiki*'s rate of fall

160

dropped to a few miles an hour and remained constant. Now there was plenty of time; it would take him days to fall all the way down to the surface of Jupiter.

But he would get there eventually, even if he did nothing about it. The balloon overhead was merely acting as an efficient parachute. It was providing no lift; nor could it do so, while the gas inside and out was the same.

With its characteristic and rather disconcerting crack the fusion reactor started up, pouring torrents of heat into the envelope overhead. Within five minutes, the rate of fall had become zero; within six, the ship had started to rise. According to the radar altimeter, it had levelled out at about two hundred and sixty-seven miles above the surface – or whatever passed for a surface on Jupiter.

Only one kind of balloon will work in an atmosphere of hydrogen, which is the lightest of all gases – and that is a hot-hydrogen balloon. As long as the fuser kept ticking over, Falcon could remain aloft, drifting across a world that could hold a hundred Pacifics. After travelling over three hundred million miles, *Kon-Tiki* had at last begun to justify her name. She was an aerial raft, adrift upon the currents of the Jovian atmosphere.

Though a whole new world was lying around him, it was more than an hour before Falcon could examine the view. First he had to check all the capsule's systems and test its response to the controls. He had to learn how much extra heat was necessary to produce a desired rate of ascent, and how much gas he must vent in order to descend. Above all, there was the question of stability. He must adjust the length of the cables attaching his capsule to the huge, pear-shaped balloon, to damp out vibrations and get the smoothest possible ride. Thus far, he was lucky; at this level, the wind was steady, and the Doppler reading on the invisible surface gave him a ground speed of two hundred and seventeen and a half miles an hour. For Jupiter, that was modest; winds of up to a thousand had been observed. But mere speed was, of course, unimportant; the real danger was turbulence. If he ran into that, only skill and experience and swift reaction could save him – and these were not matters that could yet be programmed into a computer.

Not until he was satisfied that he had got the feel of his strange craft did Falcon pay any attention to Mission Control's pleadings. Then he deployed the booms carrying the instrumentation and the atmospheric samplers. The capsule now resembled a rather untidy Christmas tree, but still rode smoothly down the Jovian winds while it radioed its torrents of information to the recorders on the ship miles above. And now, at last, he could look around ...

His first impression was unexpected, and even a little disappointing. As far as the scale of things was concerned, he might have been ballooning over an ordinary cloudscape on Earth. The horizon seemed at a normal distance; there was no feeling at all that he was on a world eleven times the diameter of his own. Then he looked at the infra-red radar, sounding the layers of atmosphere beneath him – and knew how badly his eyes had been deceived.

That layer of clouds apparently about three miles away was really more than thirty-seven miles below. And the horizon, whose distance he would have guessed at about one hundred and twenty-five, was actually eighteen hundred miles from the ship.

The crystalline clarity of the hydrohelium atmosphere and the enormous curvature of the planet had fooled him completely. It was even harder to judge distances here than on the Moon; everything he saw must be multiplied by at least ten.

It was a simple matter, and he should have been prepared for it. Yet somehow, it disturbed him profoundly. He did not feel that Jupiter was huge, but that *he* had shrunk – to a tenth of his normal size. Perhaps, with time, he would grow accustomed to the inhuman scale of this world; yet as he stared towards that unbelievably distant horizon, he felt as if a wind colder than the atmosphere around him was blowing through his soul. Despite all his arguments, this might never be a place for man. He could well be both the first and the last to descend through the clouds of Jupiter.

The sky above was almost black, except for a few wisps of ammonia cirrus perhaps twelve miles overhead. It was cold up there, on the fringes of space, but both pressure and temperature increased rapidly with depth. At the level where *Kon-Tiki* was drifting now, it was fifty below zero, and the pressure was five atmospheres. Sixty-five miles farther down, it would be as warm as equatorial Earth, and the pressure about the same as at the bottom of one of the shallower seas. Ideal conditions for life ...

A quarter of the brief Jovian day had already gone; the sun was halfway up the sky, but the light on the unbroken cloudscape below had a curious mellow quality. That extra three hundred million miles had robbed the Sun of all its power. Though the sky was clear, Falcon found himself continually thinking that it was a heavily overcast day. When night fell, the onset of darkness would be swift indeed; though it was still morning, there was a sense of autumnal twilight in the air. But autumn, of course, was something that never came to Jupiter. There were no seasons here.

Kon-Tiki had come down in the exact centre of the equatorial zone – the least colourful part of the planet. The sea of clouds that stretched out to the horizon was tinted a pale salmon; there was none of the yellows and pinks and even reds that banded Jupiter at higher altitudes. The Great Red Spot itself – most spectacular of all of the planet's features – lay thousands of miles to the south. It had been a temptation to descend there, but the south tropical disturbance was unusually active, with currents reaching over nine hundred miles an hour. It would have been asking for trouble to head into that maelstrom of unknown forces. The Great Red Spot and its mysteries would have to wait for future expeditions.

The Sun, moving across the sky twice as swiftly as it did on Earth, was now nearing the zenith and had become eclipsed by the great silver canopy of the balloon. *Kon-Tiki* was still drifting swiftly and smoothly westward at a steady two hundred and seventeen and a half, but only the radar gave any indication of this. Was it always as calm here? Falcon asked himself. The scientists who had talked learnedly of the Jovian doldrums, and had predicted that the equator would be the quietest place, seemed to know what they were talking about, after all. He had been profoundly sceptical of all such forecasts, and had agreed with one unusually modest researcher who had told him bluntly: 'There are *no* experts on Jupiter.' Well, there would be at least one by the end of this day.

If he managed to survive until then.

4. The Voices of the Deep

That first day, the Father of the Gods smiled upon him. It was as calm and peaceful here on Jupiter as it had been, years ago, when he was drifting with Webster across the plains of northern India. Falcon had time to master his new skills, until *Kon-Tiki* seemed an extension of his own body. Such luck was more than he had dared to hope for, and he began to wonder what price he might have to pay for it.

The five hours of daylight were almost over; the clouds below were full of shadows, which gave them a massive solidity they had not possessed when the Sun was higher.

Colour was swiftly draining from the sky, except in the west itself, where a band of deepening purple lay along the horizon. Above this band was the thin crescent of a closer moon, pale and bleached against the utter blackness beyond.

With a speed perceptible to the eye, the Sun went straight down over the edge of Jupiter, over eighteen hundred miles away. The stars came out in their legions – and there was the beautiful evening star of Earth, on the very frontier of twilight, reminding him how far he was from home. It followed the Sun down into the west. Man's first night on Jupiter had begun.

With the onset of darkness, *Kon-Tiki* started to sink. The balloon was no longer heated by the feeble sunlight and was losing a small part of its buoyancy. Falcon did nothing to increase lift; he had expected this and was planning to descend.

The invisible cloud deck was still over thirty miles below, and he would reach it about midnight. It showed up clearly on the infra-red radar, which also reported that it contained a vast array of complex carbon compounds, as well as the usual hydrogen, helium, and ammonia. The chemists were dying for samples of that fluffy, pinkish stuff; though some atmospheric probes had already gathered a few grams, that had only whetted their appetites. Half the basic molecules of life were here, floating high above the surface of Jupiter. And where there was food, could life be far away? That was the question that, after more than a hundred years, no one had been able to answer.

The infra-red was blocked by the clouds, but the microwave radar sliced right through and showed layer after layer, all the way down to the hidden surface almost two hundred and fifty miles below. That was barred to him by enormous pressures and temperatures; not even robot probes had ever reached it intact. It lay in tantalizing inaccessibility at the bottom of the radar screen, slightly fuzzy, and showing a curious granular structure that his equipment could not resolve.

An hour after sunset, he dropped his first probe. It fell swiftly for about sixty miles, then began to float in the denser atmosphere, sending back torrents of radio signals, which he relayed to Mission Control. Then there was nothing else to do until sunrise, except to keep an eye on the rate of descent, monitor the instruments, and answer occasional queries. While she was drifting in this steady current, *Kon-Tiki* could look after herself.

Just before midnight, a woman controller came on watch and introduced herself with the usual pleasantries. Ten minutes later she called again, her voice at once serious and excited.

'Howard! Listen in on channel forty-six – high gain.'

Channel forty-six? There were so many telemetering circuits that he knew the numbers of only those that were critical; but as soon as he threw the switch, he recognized this one. He was plugged in to the microphone on the probe, floating more than eighty miles below him in an atmosphere now almost as dense as water.

At first, there was only a soft hiss of whatever strange winds stirred down in the darkness of that unimaginable world. And then, out of the background noise, there slowly emerged a booming vibration that grew louder and louder, like the beating of a gigantic drum. It was so low that it was felt as much as heard, and the beats steadily increased their tempo, though the pitch never changed. Now it was a swift, almost infrasonic throbbing. Then, suddenly, in mid-vibration, it stopped – so abruptly that the mind could not accept the silence, but memory continued to manufacture a ghostly echo in the deepest caverns of the brain.

It was the most extraordinary sound that Falcon had ever heard, even among the multitudinous noises of Earth. He could think of no natural phenomenon that could have caused it; nor was it like the cry of any animal, not even one of the great whales ...

It came again, following exactly the same pattern. Now that he was prepared for it, he estimated the length of the sequence; from first faint throb to final crescendo, it lasted just over ten seconds.

And this time there was a real echo, very faint and far away. Perhaps it came from one of the many reflecting layers, deeper in this stratified atmosphere; perhaps it was another, more distant source. Falcon waited for a second echo, but it never came.

Mission Control reacted quickly and asked him to drop another probe at once. With two microphones operating, it would be possible to find the approximate location of the sources. Oddly enough, none of *Kon-Tiki*'s own external mikes could detect anything except wind noises. The boomings, whatever they were, must have been trapped and channelled beneath an atmospheric reflecting layer far below.

They were coming, it was soon discovered, from a cluster of sources about twelve hundred miles away. The distance gave no indication of their power; in Earth's oceans, quite feeble sounds could travel equally far. And as for the obvious assumption that living creatures were responsible, the Chief Exobiologist quickly ruled that out.

'I'll be very disappointed,' said Dr. Brenner, 'if there are no micro-organisms or plants there. But nothing like animals, because there's no free oxygen. All biochemical reactions on Jupiter must be low-energy ones – there's just no way an active creature could generate enough power to function.'

Falcon wondered if this was true; he had heard the argument before, and reserved judgment.

'In any case,' continued Brenner, 'some of those sound waves are a hundred yards long! Even an animal as big as a whale couldn't produce them. They *must* have a natural origin.'

Yes, that seemed plausible, and probably the physicists would be able to come up with an explanation. What would a blind alien make, Falcon wondered, of the sounds he might hear when standing beside a stormy sea, or a geyser, or a volcano, or a waterfall? He might well attribute them to some huge beast.

About an hour before sunrise the voices of the deep died away, and Falcon began to busy himself with preparation for the dawn of his second day. *Kon-Tiki* was now only three miles above the nearest cloud layer; the external pressure had risen to ten atmospheres, and the temperature was a tropical thirty degrees. A man could be comfortable here with no more equipment than a breathing mask and the right grade of heliox mixture.

'We've some good news for you,' Mission Control reported, soon after dawn. 'The cloud layer's breaking up. You'll have partial clearing in an hour – but watch out for turbulence.'

'I've already noticed some,' Falcon answered. 'How far down will I be able to see?'

'At least twelve miles, down to the second thermocline. *That* cloud deck is solid – it never breaks.'

And it's out of my reach, Falcon told himself; the temperature down there must be over a hundred degrees. This was the first time that any balloonist had ever had to worry, not about his ceiling, but about his basement!

Ten minutes later he could see what Mission Control had already observed from its superior vantage point. There was a change in colour near the horizon, and the cloud layer had become ragged and humpy, as if something had torn it open. He turned up his little nuclear furnace and gave *Kon-Tiki* another three miles of altitude, so that he could get a better view.

The sky below was clearing rapidly, completely, as if something was dissolving the solid overcast. An abyss was opening before his eyes. A moment later he sailed out over the edge of a cloud canyon about twelve miles deep and six hundred miles wide.

A new world lay spread beneath him; Jupiter had stripped away one of its many veils. The second layer of clouds, unattainably far below, was much darker in colour than the first. It was almost salmon pink, and curiously mottled with little islands of brick red. They were all oval-shaped, with their long axes pointing east–west, in the direction of the prevailing wind. There were hundreds of them, all about the same size, and they reminded Falcon of puffy little cumulus clouds in the terrestrial sky.

He reduced buoyancy, and *Kon-Tiki* began to drop down the face of the dissolving cliff. It was then that he noticed the snow.

White flakes were forming in the air and drifting slowly downward. Yet it was much too warm for snow – and, in any event, there was scarcely a trace of water at this altitude. Moreover, there was no glitter or sparkle about these flakes as they went cascading down into the depths. When, presently, a few landed on an instrument boom outside the main viewing port, he saw that they were a dull, opaque white – not crystalline at all – and quite large – several inches across. They looked like wax, and Falcon guessed that this was precisely what they were. Some chemical reaction was taking place in the atmosphere around him, condensing out the hydrocarbons floating in the Jovian air.

About sixty miles ahead, a disturbance was taking place in the cloud layer. The little red ovals were being jostled around, and were beginning to form a spiral – the familiar cyclonic pattern so common in the meteorology of Earth. The vortex was emerging with astonishing speed; if that was a storm ahead, Falcon told himself, he was in big trouble.

And then his concern changed to wonder – and to fear. What was developing in his line of flight was not a storm at

169

all. Something enormous – something scores of miles across – was rising through the clouds.

The reassuring thought that it, too, might be a cloud – a thunderhead boiling up from the lower levels of the atmosphere – lasted only a few seconds. No; this was *solid*. It shouldered its way through the pink-and-salmon overcast like an iceberg rising from the deeps.

An *iceberg* floating on hydrogen? That was impossible, of course; but perhaps it was not too remote an analogy. As soon as he focused the telescope upon the enigma, Falcon saw that it was a whitish, crystalline mass, threaded with streaks of red and brown. It must be, he decided, the same stuff as the 'snowflakes' falling around him – a mountain range of wax. And it was not, he soon realized, as solid as he had thought; around the edges it was continually crumbling and re-forming ...

'I know what it is,' he radioed Mission Control, which for the last few minutes had been asking anxious questions. 'It's a mass of bubbles – some kind of foam. Hydrocarbon froth. Get the chemists working on ... *Just a minute!*'

'What is it?' called Mission Control. 'What is it?'

He ignored the frantic pleas from space and concentrated all his mind upon the image in the telescope field. He had to be sure; if he made a mistake, he would be the laughing-stock of the solar system.

Then he relaxed, glanced at the clock, and switched off the nagging voice from Jupiter V.

'Hello Mission Control,' he said, very formally. 'This is Howard Falcon aboard *Kon-Tiki*. Ephemeris Time nineteen hours twenty-one minutes fifteen seconds. Latitude zero degrees five minutes North. Longitude one hundred and five degrees forty-two minutes, System One.'

'Tell Dr. Brenner that there is life on Jupiter. And it's *big* ...'

5. The Wheels of Poseidon

'I'm very happy to be proved wrong,' Dr. Brenner radioed back cheerfully. 'Nature always has something up her sleeve. Keep the long-focus camera on target and give us the steadiest pictures you can.'

The things moving up and down those waxen slopes were still too far away for Falcon to make out many details, and they must have been very large to be visible at all at such a distance. Almost black, and shaped like arrowheads, they manoeuvred by slow undulations of their entire bodies, so that they looked rather like giant manta rays, swimming above some tropical reef.

Perhaps they were sky-borne cattle, browsing on the cloud pastures of Jupiter, for they seemed to be feeding along the dark, red-brown streaks that ran like dried-up river beds down the flanks of the floating cliffs. Occasionally, one of them would dive headlong into the mountain of foam and disappear completely from sight.

Kon-Tiki was moving only slowly with respect to the cloud layer below; it would be at least three hours before she was above those ephemeral hills. She was in a race with the Sun. Falcon hoped that darkness would not fall before he could get a good view of the mantas, as he had christened them, as well as the fragile landscape over which they flapped their way.

It was a long three hours. During the whole time, he kept the external microphones on full gain, wondering if here was the source of that booming in the night. The mantas were certainly large enough to have produced it; when he could get an accurate measurement, he discovered that they were almost a hundred yards across the wings. That was three times the length of the largest whale – though he doubted if they could weigh more than a few tons.

171

Half an hour before sunset, *Kon-Tiki* was almost above the 'mountains'.

'No,' said Falcon, answering Mission Control's repeated questions about the mantas, 'they're still showing no reaction to me. I don't think they're intelligent – they look like harmless vegetarians. And even if they try to chase me, I'm sure they can't reach my altitude.'

Yet he was a little disappointed when the mantas showed not the slightest interest in him as he sailed high above their feeding ground. Perhaps they had no way of detecting his presence. When he examined and photographed them through the telescope, he could see no signs of any sense organs. The creatures were simply huge black deltas, rippling over hills and valleys that, in reality, were little more substantial than the clouds of Earth. Though they looked solid, Falcon knew that anyone who stepped on those white mountains would go crashing through them as if they were made of tissue paper.

At close quarters he could see the myriads of cellules or bubbles from which they were formed. Some of these were quite large – a yard or so in diameter – and Falcon wondered in what witches' cauldron of hydrocarbons they had been brewed. There must be enough petrochemicals deep down in the atmosphere of Jupiter to supply all Earth's needs for a million years.

The short day had almost gone when he passed over the crest of the waxen hills, and the light was fading rapidly along their lower slopes. There were no mantas on this western side, and for some reason the topography was very different. The foam was sculptured into long, level terraces, like the interior of a lunar crater. He could almost imagine that they were gigantic steps leading down to the hidden surface of the planet.

And on the lowest of those steps, just clear of the swirling clouds that the mountain had displaced when it came surging skyward, was a roughly oval mass, one or two miles across. It was difficult to see, since it was only a little darker than the grey-white foam on which it rested. Falcon's first thought was that he was looking at a forest of pallid trees, like giant mushrooms that had never seen the Sun.

Yes, it must be a forest – he could see hundreds of thin trunks, springing from the white waxy froth in which they were rooted. But the trees were packed astonishingly close together; there was scarcely any space between them. Perhaps it was not a forest, after all, but a single enormous tree – like one of the giant multi-trunked banyans of the East. Once he had seen a banyan tree in Java that was over six hundred and fifty yards across; this monster was at least ten times that size.

The light had almost gone. The cloudscape had turned purple with refracted sunlight, and in a few seconds that, too, would have vanished. In the last light of his second day on Jupiter, Howard Falcon saw – or thought he saw – something that cast the gravest doubts on his interpretation of the white oval.

Unless the dim light had totally deceived him, those hundreds of thin trunks were beating back and forth, in perfect synchronism, like fronds of kelp rocking in the surge.

And the tree was no longer in the place where he had first seen it.

'Sorry about this,' said Mission Control, soon after sunset, 'but we think Source Beta is going to blow within the next hour. Probability seventy per cent.'

Falcon glanced quickly at the chart. Beta – Jupiter latitude one hundred and forty degrees – was over eighteen thousand six hundred miles away and well below his horizon. Even though major eruptions ran as high as ten megatons, he was much too far away for the shock wave to be a serious danger. The radio storm that it would trigger was, however, quite a different matter.

The decameter outbursts that sometimes made Jupiter the most powerful radio source in the whole sky had been discovered back in the 1950s, to the utter astonishment of the astronomers. Now, more than a century later, their real cause was still a mystery. Only the symptoms were understood; the explanation was completely unknown.

The 'volcano' theory had best stood the test of time, although no one imagined that this word had the same meaning on Jupiter as on Earth. At frequent intervals – often several times a day – titanic eruptions occurred in the lower depths of the atmosphere, probably on the hidden surface of the planet itself. A great column of gas, more than six hundred miles high, would start boiling upward as if determined to escape into space.

Against the most powerful gravitational field of all the planets, it had no chance. Yet some traces – a mere few million tons – usually managed to reach the Jovian atmosphere; and when they did, all hell broke loose.

The radiation belts surrounding Jupiter completely dwarf the feeble Van Allen belts of Earth. When they are short-circuited by an ascending column of gas, the result is an electrical discharge millions of times more powerful than any terrestrial flash of lightning; it sends a colossal thunderclap of radio noise flooding across the entire solar system and on out to the stars.

It had been discovered that these radio outbursts came from four main areas of the planet. Perhaps there were weaknesses there that allowed the fires of the interior to break out from time to time. The scientists on Ganymede, largest of Jupiter's many moons, now thought that they could predict the onset of a decameter storm; their accuracy was about as good as a weather forecaster's of the early 1900s.

Falcon did not know whether to welcome or to fear a

radio storm; it would certainly add to the value of the mission – if he survived it. His course had been planned to keep as far as possible from the main centres of disturbance, especially the most active one, Source Alpha. As luck would have it, the threatening Beta was the closest to him. He hoped that the distance, almost three-fourths the circumference of Earth, was safe enough.

'Probability ninety per cent,' said Mission Control with a distinct note of urgency. 'And forget that hour. Ganymede says it may be any moment.'

The radio had scarcely fallen silent when the reading on the magnetic field-strength meter started to shoot upward. Before it could go off scale, it reversed and began to drop as rapidly as it had risen. Far away and thousands of miles below, something had given the planet's molten core a titanic jolt.

'There she blows!' called Mission Control.

'Thanks, I already know. When will the storm hit me?'

'You can expect onset in five minutes. Peak in ten.'

Far around the curve of Jupiter, a funnel of gas as wide as the Pacific Ocean was climbing spaceward at thousands of miles an hour. Already, the thunderstorms of the lower atmosphere would be raging around it – but they were nothing compared with the fury that would explode when the radiation belt was reached and began dumping its surplus electrons on to the planet. Falcon began to retract all the instrument booms that were extended out from the capsule. There were no other precautions he could take. It would be four hours before the atmospheric shock wave reached him – but the radio blast, travelling at the speed of light, would be here in a tenth of a second, once the discharge had been triggered.

The radio monitor, scanning back and forth across the spectrum, still showed nothing unusual, just the normal mush of background static. Then Falcon noticed that the noise level was slowly creeping upward. The explosion was gathering its strength.

At such a distance he had never expected to *see* anything. But suddenly a flicker as of far-off heat lightning danced along the eastern horizon. Simultaneously, half the circuit breakers jumped out of the main switchboard, the lights failed and all communications channels went dead.

He tried to move, but was completely unable to do so. The paralysis that gripped him was not merely psychological; he seemed to have lost all control of his limbs and could feel a painful tingling sensation over his entire body. It was impossible that the electric field could have penetrated this shielded cabin. Yet there was a flickering glow over the instrument board, and he could hear the unmistakable crackle of a brush discharge.

With a series of sharp bangs, the emergency systems went into operation, and the overloads reset themselves. The lights flickered on again. And Falcon's paralysis disappeared as swiftly as it had come.

After glancing at the board to make sure that all circuits were back to normal, he moved quickly to the viewing ports.

There was no need to switch on the inspection lamps – the cables supporting the capsule seemed to be on fire. Lines of light glowing an electric blue against the darkness stretched upward from the main lift ring to the equator of the giant balloon; and rolling slowly along several of them were dazzling balls of fire.

The sight was so strange and so beautiful that it was hard to read any menace in it. Few people, Falcon knew, had ever seen ball lightning from such close quarters – and certainly none had survived if they were riding a hydrogen-filled balloon back in the atmosphere of Earth. He remembered the flaming death of the *Hindenburg*, destroyed by a stray spark when she docked at Lakehurst in 1937; as she had done so often in the past. The horrifying old newsreel film flashed through his mind. But at least that could not happen here, though there was more hydrogen above his head than had ever filled the last of the Zeppelins. It would be a few billion years yet, before anyone could light a fire in the atmosphere of Jupiter.

With a sound like briskly frying bacon, the speech circuit came back to life.

'Hello, *Kon-Tiki* – are you receiving? Are you receiving?'

The words were chopped and badly distorted, but intelligible. Falcon's spirits lifted; he had resumed contact with the world of men.

'I receive you,' he said. 'Quite an electrical display, but no damage – so far.'

'Thanks – thought we'd lost you. Please check telemetry channels three, seven, twenty-six. Also gain on camera two. And we don't quite believe the readings on the external ionization probes ...'

Reluctantly Falcon tore his gaze away from the fascinating pyrotechnic display around *Kon-Tiki*, though from time to time he kept glancing out of the windows. The ball lightning disappeared first, the fiery globes slowly expanding until they reached a critical size, at which they vanished in a gentle explosion. But even an hour later, there were still faint glows around all the exposed metal on the outside of the capsule; and the radio circuits remained noisy until well after midnight.

The remaining hours of darkness were completely uneventful – until just before dawn. Because it came from the east, Falcon assumed that he was seeing the first faint hint of sunrise. Then he realized that it was twenty minutes too early for this – and the glow that had appeared along the horizon was moving towards him even as he watched. It swiftly detached itself from the arch of stars that marked the invisible edge of the planet, and he saw that it was a relatively narrow band, quite sharply defined. The beam of an enormous searchlight appeared to be swinging beneath the clouds.

Perhaps sixty miles behind the first racing bar of light came another, parallel to it and moving at the same speed. And beyond that another, and another – until all the sky flickered with alternating sheets of light and darkness.

By this time, Falcon thought, he had been inured to wonders, and it seemed impossible that this display of pure, soundless luminosity could present the slightest danger. But it was so astonishing, and so inexplicable, that he felt cold, naked fear gnawing at his self-control. No man could look upon such a sight without feeling like a helpless pygmy in the presence of forces beyond his comprehension. Was it possible that, after all, Jupiter carried not only life but also intelligence? And, perhaps, an intelligence that only now was beginning to react to his alien presence?

'Yes, we see it,' said Mission Control, in a voice that echoed his own awe. 'We've no idea what it is. Stand by, we're calling Ganymede.'

The display was slowly fading; the bands racing in from the far horizon were much fainter, as if the energies that powered them were becoming exhausted. In five minutes it was all over; the last faint pulse of light flickered along the western sky and then was gone. Its passing left Falcon with an overwhelming sense of relief. The sight was so hypnotic, and so disturbing, that it was not good for any man's peace of mind to contemplate it too long.

He was more shaken than he cared to admit. The electrical storm was something that he could understand; but *this* was totally incomprehensible.

Mission Control was still silent. He knew that the information banks up on Ganymede were now being searched as men and computers turned their minds to the problem. If no answer could be found there, it would be necessary to call Earth; that would mean a delay of almost an hour. The possibility that even Earth might be unable to help was one that Falcon did not care to contemplate.

He had never before been so glad to hear the voice of Mission Control as when Dr. Brenner finally came on the circuit. The biologist sounded relieved, yet subdued – like a man who has just come through some great intellectual crisis.

'Hello, *Kon-Tiki.* We've solved your problem, but we can still hardly believe it.

'What you've been seeing is bioluminescence, very similar to that produced by micro-organisms in the tropical seas of Earth. Here they're in the atmosphere, not the ocean, but the principle is the same.'

'But the pattern,' protested Falcon, 'was so regular – so *artificial.* And it was hundreds of miles across!'

'It was even larger than you imagine; you observed only a small part of it. The whole pattern was over three thousand miles wide and looked like a revolving wheel. You merely saw the spokes, sweeping past you at about six-tenths of a mile a second . . .'

'A *second*!' Falcon could not help interjecting. 'No animals could move that fast!'

'Of course not. Let me explain. What you saw was triggered by the shock wave from Source Beta, moving at the speed of sound.'

'But what about the pattern?' Falcon insisted.

'That's the surprising part. It's a very rare phenomenon, but identical wheels of light – except that they're a thousand times smaller – have been observed in the Persian Gulf and the Indian Ocean. Listen to this: British India Company's *Patna*, Persian Gulf, May 1880, 11.30 p.m. – "an enormous luminous wheel, whirling round, the spokes of which appeared to brush the ship along. The spokes were 200 or 300 yards long . . . each wheel contained about sixteen

179

spokes ..." And here's one from the Gulf of Omar, dated May 23rd, 1906: "The intensely bright luminescence approached us rapidly, shooting sharply defined light rays to the west in rapid succession, like the beam from the searchlight of a warship ... To the left of us, a gigantic fiery wheel formed itself, with spokes that reached as far as one could see. The whole wheel whirled around for two or three minutes ..." The archive computer on Ganymede dug up about five hundred cases. It would have printed out the lot if we hadn't stopped it in time.'

'I'm convinced – but still baffled.'

'I don't blame you. The full explanation wasn't worked out until late in the twentieth century. It seems that these luminous wheels are the results of submarine earthquakes, and always occur in shallow waters where the shock waves can be reflected and cause standing wave patterns. Sometimes bars, sometimes rotating wheels – the "Wheels of Poseidon", they've been called. The theory was finally proved by making underwater explosions and photographing the results from a satellite. No wonder sailors used to be superstitious. Who would have believed a thing like *this*?'

So that was it, Falcon told himself. When Source Beta blew its top, it must have sent shock waves in all directions – through the compressed gas of the lower atmosphere, through the solid body of Jupiter itself. Meeting and crisscrossing, those waves must have cancelled here, reinforced there; the whole planet must have rung like a bell.

Yet the explanation did not destroy the sense of wonder and awe; he would never be able to forget those flickering bands of light, racing through the unattainable depths of the Jovian atmosphere. He felt that he was not merely on a strange planet, but in some magical realm between myth and reality.

This was a world where absolutely *anything* could happen, and no man could possibly guess what the future would bring.

And he still had a whole day to go.

6. MEDUSA

When the true dawn finally arrived, it brought a·sudden change of weather. *Kon-Tiki* was moving through a blizzard; waxen snowflakes were falling so thickly that visibility was reduced to zero. Falcon began to worry about the weight that might be accumulating on the envelope. Then he noticed that any flakes settling outside the windows quickly disappeared; *Kon-Tiki*'s continual outpouring of heat was evaporating them as swiftly as they arrived.

If he had been ballooning on Earth, he would also have worried about the possibility of collision. At least that was no danger here; any Jovian mountains were several hundred miles below him. And as for the floating islands of foam, hitting them would probably be like ploughing into slightly hardened soap bubbles.

Nevertheless, he switched on the horizontal radar, which until now had been completely useless; only the vertical beam, giving his distance from the invisible surface, had thus far been°of any value. Then he had another surprise.

Scattered across a huge sector of the sky ahead were dozens of large and brilliant echoes. They were completely isolated from one another and apparently hung unsupported in space. Falcon remembered a phrase the earliest aviators had used to describe one of the hazards of their profession: 'clouds stuffed with rocks'. That was a perfect description of what seemed to lie in the track of *Kon-Tiki*.

It was a disconcerting sight; then Falcon again reminded himself that nothing *really* solid could possibly hover in this atmosphere. Perhaps it was some strange meteorological phenomenon. In any case, the nearest echo was about a hundred and twenty-five miles.

He reported to Mission Control, which could provide no explanation. But it gave the welcome news that he would be clear of the blizzard in another thirty minutes.

It did not warn him, however, of the violent cross-wind that abruptly grabbed *Kon-Tiki* and swept it almost at right angles to its previous track. Falcon needed all his skill and the maximum use of what little control he had over his ungainly vehicle to prevent it from being capsized. Within minutes he was racing northward at over three hundred miles an hour. Then, as suddenly as it had started, the turbulence ceased; he was still moving at high speed, but in smooth air. He wondered if he had been caught in the Jovian equivalent of a jet stream.

The snow storm dissolved; and he saw what Jupiter had been preparing for him.

Kon-Tiki had entered the funnel of a gigantic whirlpool, some six hundred miles across. The balloon was being swept along a curving wall of cloud. Overhead, the sun was shining in a clear sky; but far beneath, this great hole in the atmosphere drilled down to unknown depths until it reached a misty floor where lightning flickered almost continuously.

Though the vessel was being dragged downward so slowly that it was in no immediate danger, Falcon increased the flow of heat into the envelope until *Kon-Tiki* hovered at a constant altitude. Not until then did he abandon the fantastic spectacle outside and consider again the problem of the radar.

The nearest echo was now only about twenty-five miles away. All of them, he quickly realized, were distributed along the wall of the vortex, and were moving with it, apparently caught in the whirlpool like *Kon-Tiki* itself. He aimed the telescope along the radar bearing and found himself looking at a curious mottled cloud that almost filled the field of view.

It was not easy to see, being only a little darker than the whirling wall of mist that formed its background. Not until he had been staring for several minutes did Falcon realize that he had met it once before.

The first time it had been crawling across the drifting mountains of foam, and he had mistaken it for a giant, many-trunked tree. Now at last he could appreciate its real size and complexity and could give it a better name to fix its image in his mind. It did not resemble a tree at all, but a jellyfish – a medusa, such as might be met trailing its tentacles as it drifted along the warm eddies of the Gulf Stream.

This medusa was more than a mile across and its scores of dangling tentacles were hundreds of feet long. They swayed slowly back and forth in perfect unison, taking more than a minute for each complete undulation – almost as if the creature was clumsily rowing itself through the sky.

The other echoes were more distant medusae. Falcon focused the telescope on half a dozen and could see no variations in shape or size. They all seemed to be of the same species, and he wondered just why they were drifting lazily around in this six-hundred-mile orbit. Perhaps they were feeding upon the aerial plankton sucked in by the whirlpool, as *Kon-Tiki* itself had been.

'Do you realize, Howard,' said Dr. Brenner, when he had recovered from his initial astonishment, 'that this thing is about a hundred thousand times as large as the biggest whale? And even if it's only a gasbag, it must still weigh a million tons! I can't even guess at its metabolism. It must generate megawatts of heat to maintain its buoyancy.'

'But if it's just a gasbag, why is it such a damn good radar reflector?'

'I haven't the faintest idea. Can you get any closer?'

Brenner's question was not an idle one. If he changed altitude to take advantage of the differing wind velocities,

Falcon could approach the medusa as closely as he wished. At the moment, however, he preferred his present twenty-five miles and said so, firmly.

'I see what you mean,' Brenner answered, a little reluctantly. 'Let's stay where we are for the present.' That 'we' gave Falcon a certain wry amusement; an extra sixty thousand miles made a considerable difference in one's point of view.

For the next two hours *Kon-Tiki* drifted uneventfully in the gyre of the great whirlpool, while Falcon experimented with filters and camera contrast, trying to get a clear view of the medusa. He began to wonder if its elusive colouration was some kind of camouflage; perhaps, like many animals of Earth, it was trying to lose itself against its background. That was a trick used by both hunters and hunted.

In which category was the medusa? That was a question he could hardly expect to have answered in the short time that was left to him. Yet just before noon, without the slightest warning, the answer came ...

Like a squadron of antique jet fighters, five mantas came sweeping through the wall of mist that formed the funnel of the vortex. They were flying in a V formation directly towards the pallid grey cloud of the medusa; and there was no doubt, in Falcon's mind, that they were on the attack. He had been quite wrong to assume that they were harmless vegetarians.

Yet everything happened at such a leisurely pace that it was like watching a slow-motion film. The mantas undulated along at perhaps thirty miles an hour; it seemed ages before they reached the medusa, which continued to paddle imperturbably along at an even slower speed. Huge though they were, the mantas looked tiny beside the monster they were approaching. When they flapped down on its back, they appeared about as large as birds landing on a whale.

Could the medusa defend itself, Falcon wondered. He did not see how the attacking mantas could be in danger as long as they avoided those huge clumsy tentacles. And perhaps their host was not even aware of them; they could be insignificant parasites, tolerated as are fleas upon a dog.

But now it was obvious that the medusa was in distress. With agonizing slowness, it began to tip over like a capsizing ship. After ten minutes it had tilted forty-five degrees; it was also rapidly losing altitude. It was impossible not to feel a sense of pity for the beleaguered monster, and to Falcon the sight brought bitter memories. In a grotesque way, the fall of the medusa was almost a parody of the dying *Queen*'s last moments.

Yet he knew that his sympathies were on the wrong side. High intelligence could develop only among predators – not among the drifting browsers of either sea or air. The mantas were far closer to him than was this monstrous bag of gas. And anyway, who could *really* sympathize with a creature a hundred thousand times larger than a whale?

Then he noticed that the medusa's tactics seemed to be having some effect. The mantas had been disturbed by its slow roll and were flapping heavily away from its back – like gorged vultures interrupted at mealtime. But they did not move very far, continuing to hover a few yards from the still-capsizing monster.

There was a sudden, blinding flash of light synchronized with a crash of static over the radio. One of the mantas, slowly twisting end over end, was plummeting straight downward. As it fell, a plume of black smoke trailed behind it. The resemblance to an aircraft going down in flames was quite uncanny.

In unison, the remaining mantas dived steeply away from the medusa, gaining speed by losing altitude. They had, within minutes, vanished back into the wall of cloud from which they had emerged. And the medusa, no longer falling, began to roll back towards the horizontal. Soon it was sailing along once more on an even keel, as if nothing had happened.

'Beautiful!' said Dr. Brenner, after a moment of stunned silence. 'It's developed electric defences, like some of our eels and rays. But that must have been about a million volts! Can you see any organs that might produce the discharge? Anything looking like electrodes?'

'No,' Falcon answered, after switching to the highest power of the telescope. 'But here's something odd. Do you see this pattern? Check back on the earlier images. I'm sure it wasn't there before.'

A broad, mottled band had appeared along the side of the medusa. It formed a startlingly regular checkerboard, each square of which was itself speckled in a complex sub-pattern of short horizontal lines. They were spaced at equal distances in a geometrically perfect array of rows and columns.

'You're right,' said Dr. Brenner, with something very much like awe in his voice. 'That's just appeared. And I'm afraid to tell you what I think it is.'

'Well, I have no reputation to lose – at least as a biologist. Shall I give my guess?'

'Go ahead.'

'That's a large meter-band radio array. The sort of thing they used back at the beginning of the twentieth century.'

'I was afraid you'd say that. Now we know why it gave such a massive echo.'

'But why has it just appeared?'

'Probably an after effect of the discharge.'

'I've just had another thought,' said Falcon, rather slowly. 'Do you suppose it's *listening* to us?'

'On this frequency? I doubt it. Those are meter – no, *decameter* antennas – judging by their size. Hmm ... that's an idea!'

Dr. Brenner fell silent, obviously contemplating some new line of thought. Presently he continued: 'I bet they're tuned to the radio outbursts! That's something nature never got around to doing on Earth.... We have animals with sonar and even electric sense, but nothing ever developed a radio sense. Why bother where there was so much light?

'But it's different here. Jupiter is *drenched* with radio energy. It's worth while using it – maybe even tapping it. That thing could be a floating power plant!'

A new voice cut into the conversation.

'Mission Commander here. This is all very interesting, but there's a much more important matter to settle. *Is it intelligent?* If so, we've got to consider the First Contact directives.'

'Until I came here,' said Dr. Brenner, somewhat ruefully, 'I would have sworn that anything that could make a short-wave antenna system *must* be intelligent. Now, I'm not sure. This could have evolved naturally. I suppose it's no more fantastic than the human eye.'

'Then we have to play safe and assume intelligence. For the present, therefore, this expedition comes under all the clauses of the Prime directive.'

There was a long silence while everyone on the radio circuit absorbed the implications of this. For the first time in the history of space flight, the rules that had been established through more than a century of argument might have to be applied. Man had – it was hoped – profited from his mistakes on Earth. Not only moral considerations, but also his own self-interest demanded that he should not repeat them among the planets. It could be disastrous to treat a superior intelligence as the American settlers had treated the Indians, or as almost everyone had treated the Africans ...

The first rule was: keep your distance. Make no attempt to approach, or even to communicate, until 'they' have had plenty of time to study you. Exactly what was meant by 'plenty of time', no one had ever been able to decide. It was left to the discretion of the man on the spot.

A responsibility of which he had never dreamed had descended upon Howard Falcon. In the few hours that remained to him on Jupiter, he might become the first ambassador of the human race.

And *that* was an irony so delicious that he almost wished the surgeons had restored to him the power of laughter.

7. PRIME DIRECTIVE

It was growing darker, but Falcon scarcely noticed as he strained his eyes towards that living cloud in the field of the telescope. The wind that was steadily sweeping *Kon-Tiki* around the funnel of the great whirlpool had now brought him within twelve miles of the creature. If he got much closer than six, he would take evasive action. Though he felt certain that the medusa's electric weapons were short ranged, he did not wish to put the matter to the test. That would be a problem for future explorers, and he wished them luck.

Now it was quite dark in the capsule. That was strange, because sunset was still hours away. Automatically, he glanced at the horizontally scanning radar, as he had done every few minutes. Apart from the medusa he was studying, there was no other object within sixty miles of him.

Suddenly, with startling power, he heard the sound that had come booming out of the Jovian night – the throbbing beat that grew more and more rapid, then stopped in mid-crescendo. The whole capsule vibrated with it like a pea in a kettledrum.

Falcon realized two things almost simultaneously during the sudden, aching silence. *This* time the sound was not coming from thousands of miles away, over a radio circuit. It was in the very atmosphere around him.

The second thought was even more disturbing. He had quite forgotten – it was inexcusable, but there had been other apparently more important things on his mind – that most of the sky above him was completely blanked out by *Kon Tiki*'s gasbag. Being lightly silvered to conserve its heat, the great balloon was an effective shield both to radar and to vision.

He had known this, of course; it had been a minor defect of the design, tolerated because it did not appear important. It seemed very important to Howard Falcon now – as he saw that fence of gigantic tentacles, thicker than the trunks of any tree, descending all around the capsule.

He heard Brenner yelling: 'Remember the Prime directive! Don't alarm it!' Before he could make an appropriate answer that overwhelming drumbeat started again and drowned all other sounds.

The sign of a really skilled test pilot is how he reacts not to foreseeable emergencies, but to ones that nobody could have anticipated. Falcon did not hesitate for more than a second to analyse the situation. In a lightning-swift movement, he pulled the rip cord.

That word was an archaic survival from the days of the first hydrogen balloons; on *Kon-Tiki*, the rip cord did not tear open the gasbag, but merely operated a set of louvers around the upper curve of the envelope. At once the hot gas started to rush out; *Kon-Tiki*, deprived of her lift, began to fall swiftly in this gravity field two and a half miles as strong as Earth's.

Falcon had a momentary glimpse of great tentacles whipping upward and away. He had just time to note that they were studded with large bladders or sacs, presumably to give them buoyancy, and that they ended in multitudes of thin feelers like the roots of a plant. He half expected a bolt of lightning –but nothing happened.

His precipitous rate of descent was slackening as the atmosphere thickened and the deflated envelope acted as a parachute. When *Kon-Tiki* had dropped about two miles, he felt that it was safe to close the louvers again. By the time he had restored buoyancy and was in equilibrium once more, he had lost another mile of altitude and was getting dangerously near his safety limit.

He peered anxiously through the overhead windows, though he did not expect to see anything except the obscuring bulk of the balloon. But he had sideslipped during his descent, and part of the medusa was just visible a couple of miles above him. It was much closer than he expected – and it was still coming down, faster than he would have believed possible.

Mission Control was calling anxiously. He shouted: 'I'm O.K. – but it's still coming after me. I can't go any deeper.'

That was not quite true. He could go a lot deeper – about one hundred and eighty miles. But it would be a one-way trip, and most of the journey would be of little interest to him.

Then, to his great relief, he saw that the medusa was levelling off, not quite a mile above him. Perhaps it had decided to approach this strange intruder with caution; or perhaps it, too, found this deeper layer uncomfortably hot. The temperature was over fifty degrees centigrade, and Falcon wondered how much longer his life-support system could handle matters.

Dr. Brenner was back on the circuit, still worrying about the Prime directive.

'Remember – it may only be inquisitive!' he cried, without much conviction. 'Try not to frighten it!'

Falcon was getting rather tired of this advice and recalled a TV discussion he had once seen between a space lawyer and an astronaut. After the full implications of the Prime directive had been carefully spelled out, the incredulous spacer had exclaimed: 'Then if there was no alternative, I must sit still and let myself be eaten?' The lawyer had not even cracked a smile when he answered: 'That's an *excellent* summing up.'

It had seemed funny at the time; it was not at all amusing now.

And then Falcon saw something that made him even more unhappy. The medusa was still hovering about a mile above him – but one of its tentacles was becoming incredibly elongated, and was stretching down towards *Kon-Tiki*, thinning out at the same time. As a boy he had once seen the funnel of a tornado descending from a storm cloud over the Kansas plains. The thing coming towards him now evoked vivid memories of that black, twisting snake in the sky.

'I'm rapidly running out of options,' he reported to Mission Control. 'I now have a choice between frightening it – and giving it a bad stomach-ache. I don't think it will find *Kon-Tiki* very digestible, if that's what it has in mind.'

He waited for comments from Brenner, but the biologist remained silent.

'Very well. It's twenty-seven minutes ahead of time, but I'm starting the ignition sequencer. I hope I'll have enough reserve to correct my orbit later.'

He could no longer see the medusa; once more it was directly overhead. But he knew the descending tentacle must now be very close to the balloon. It would take almost five minutes to bring the reactor up to full thrust ...

The fusor was primed. The orbit computer had not rejected the situation as wholly impossible. The air scoops were open, ready to gulp in tons of the surrounding hydrohelium on demand. Even under optimum conditions, this

191

would have been the moment of truth – for there had been no way of testing how a nuclear ramjet would *really* work in the strange atmosphere of Jupiter.

Very gently something rocked *Kon-Tiki*. Falcon tried to ignore it.

Ignition had been planned at six miles higher, in an atmosphere of less than a quarter of the density and thirty degrees cooler. Too bad.

What was the shallowest dive he could get away with, for the air scoops to work? When the ram ignited, he'd be heading towards Jupiter with two and a half g's to help him get there. Could he possibly pull out in time?

A large, heavy hand patted the balloon. The whole vessel bobbed up and down, like one of the yo-yo's that had just become the craze on Earth.

Of course, Brenner *might* be perfectly right. Perhaps it was just trying to be friendly. Maybe he should try to talk to it over the radio. Which should it be: 'Pretty pussy'? 'Down, Fido'? Or 'Take me to your leader'?

The tritium-deuterium ratio was correct. He was ready to light the candle, with a hundred-million-degree match.

The thin tip of the tentacle came slithering around the edge of the balloon some sixty yards away. It was about the size of an elephant's trunk, and by the delicate way it was moving appeared to be almost as sensitive. There were little palps at its end, like questing mouths. He was sure that Dr. Brenner would be fascinated.

This seemed about as good a time as any. He gave a swift scan of the entire control board, started the final four-second ignition count, broke the safety seal, and pressed the JETTISON switch.

There was a sharp explosion and an instant loss of weight. *Kon-Tiki* was falling freely, nose down. Overhead, the discarded balloon was racing upward, dragging the inquisitive tentacle with it. Falcon had no time to see if the gasbag actually hit the medusa, because at that moment the ramjet fired and he had other matters to think about.

A roaring column of hot hydrohelium was pouring out of the reactor nozzles, swiftly building up thrust – but *towards* Jupiter, not away from it. He could not pull out yet, for vector control was too sluggish. Unless he could gain complete control and achieve horizontal flight within the next five seconds, the vehicle would dive too deeply into the atmosphere and would be destroyed.

With agonizing slowness – those five seconds seemed like fifty – he managed to flatten out, then pull the nose upward. He glanced back only once and caught a final glimpse of the medusa, many miles away. *Kon-Tiki*'s discarded gasbag had apparently escaped from its grasp, for he could see no sign of it.

Now he was master once more – no longer drifting helplessly on the winds of Jupiter, but riding his own column of atomic fire back to the stars. He was confident that the ramjet would steadily give him velocity and altitude until he had reached near-orbital speed at the fringes of the atmosphere. Then, with a brief burst of pure rocket power, he would regain the freedom of space.

Halfway to orbit, he looked south and saw the tremendous enigma of the Great Red Spot – that floating island twice the size of Earth – coming up over the horizon. He stared into its mysterious beauty until the computer warned him that conversion to rocket thrust was only sixty seconds ahead. He tore his gaze reluctantly away.

'Some other time,' he murmured.

'What's that?' said Mission Control. 'What did you say?'

'It doesn't matter,' he replied.

'You're a hero now, Howard,' said Webster, 'not just a celebrity. You've given them something to think about – injected some excitement into their lives. Not one in a million will actually travel to the Outer Giants, but the whole human race will go in imagination. And that's what counts.'

'I'm glad to have made your job a little easier.'

Webster was too old a friend to take offence at the note of irony. Yet it surprised him. And this was not the first change in Howard that he had noticed since the return from Jupiter.

The Administrator pointed to the famous sign on his desk, borrowed from an impresario of an earlier age: ASTONISH ME!

'I'm not ashamed of my job. New knowledge, new resources – they're all very well. But men also need novelty and excitement. Space travel has become routine; you've made it a great adventure once more. It will be a long, long time before we get Jupiter pigeonholed. And maybe longer still before we understand those medusae. I still think that one *knew* where your blind spot was. Anyway, have you decided on your next move? Saturn, Uranus, Neptune – you name it.'

'I don't know. I've thought about Saturn, but I'm not really needed there. It's only one gravity, not two and a half like Jupiter. So men can handle it.'

Men, thought Webster. He said 'men'. He's never done that before. And when did I last hear him use the word 'we'? He's changing, slipping away from us ...

'Well,' he said aloud, rising from his chair to conceal his slight uneasiness, 'let's get the conference started. The cameras are all set up and everyone's waiting. You'll meet a lot of old friends.'

He stressed the last word, but Howard showed no response. The leathery mask of his face was becoming more and more difficult to read. Instead, he rolled back from the Administrator's desk, unlocked his undercarriage so that it no longer formed a chair, and rose on his hydraulics to his full seven feet of height. It had been good psychology on the part of the surgeons to give him that extra twelve inches, to compensate somewhat for all that he had lost when the *Queen* had crashed.

Falcon waited until Webster had opened the door, then pivoted neatly on his balloon tyres and headed for it at a smooth and silent twenty miles an hour. The display of speed and precision was not flaunted arrogantly; rather, it had become quite unconscious.

Howard Falcon, who had once been a man and could still pass for one over a voice circuit, felt a calm sense of achievement – and, for the first time in years, something like peace of mind. Since his return from Jupiter, the nightmares had ceased. He had found his role at last.

He now knew why he had dreamed about that superchimp aboard the doomed *Queen Elizabeth*. Neither man nor beast, it was between two worlds; and so was he.

He alone could travel unprotected on the lunar surface. The life-support system inside the metal cylinder that had replaced his fragile body functioned equally well in space or under water. Gravity fields ten times that of Earth were an inconvenience, but nothing more. And no gravity was best of all ...

The human race was becoming more remote, the ties of kinship more tenuous. Perhaps these air-breathing, radiation-sensitive bundles of unstable carbon compounds had no right beyond the atmosphere; they should stick to their natural homes – Earth, Moon, Mars.

Some day the real masters of space would be machines,

not men – and he was neither. Already conscious of his destiny, he took a sombre pride in his unique loneliness – the first immortal midway between two orders of creation.

He would, after all, be an ambassador; between the old and the new – between the creatures of carbon and the creatures of metal who must one day supersede them.

Both would have need of him in the troubled centuries that lay ahead.

THE SCIENCE FICTION BOOKS
OF ARTHUR C. CLARKE

THE books are listed in chronological order of publication. The publisher of the first World edition is given, and where this was an American edition this is indicated by (US). Following this, all British editions are listed.

Short stories are indicated by 'collection', Omnibus Editions have a list of contents and these are cross-indexed by the use of In: references. All re-issues of a book under a different title are listed with the original title.

Books published in hardcover are indicated by (hd) while all others are paperbacks. The date for each edition is also given. An asterisk (*) indicates that the edition was in print when this list was revised in 1976.

BIBLIOGRAPHY

THE SANDS OF MARS
> Sidgwick & Jackson (hd), 1951*; Corgi, 1954; Pan, 1964; Sphere, 1969; Thorpe (hd, Large print), 1971; Sidgwick & Jackson, 1976*.
> In: *Prelude to Mars*, 1965 (US hd), and *A Second Arthur Clarke Omnibus*, 1968 (hd).

ISLANDS IN THE SKY
> Winston (US hd), 1952; Sidgwick & Jackson (hd), 1952*; Digit, 1964; Puffin (Penguin), 1972*.

CHILDHOOD'S END
> Ballantine (US hd/paper), 1953; Sidgwick & Jackson (hd), 1955*; Science Fiction Book Club (hd), 1955; Pan, 1956*.

In: *Across the Sea of Stars*, 1959, and *An Arthur Clarke Omnibus*, 1965.

AGAINST THE FALL OF NIGHT

Gnome Press (US hd), 1953.

In: *The Lion of Comarre and Against the Fall of Night*, 1968.

Expanded as: *The City and the Stars*, 1956.

EXPEDITION TO EARTH (collection)

Ballantine (US hd/paper), 1953; Sidgwick & Jackson (hd), 1954*; Corgi, 1959; Pan, 1966; Sphere, 1968*.

PRELUDE TO SPACE

Galaxy S.F., 1951; Sidgwick & Jackson (hd), 1953*; Pan, 1954; New English Library, 1962.

In: *An Arthur Clarke Omnibus*, 1965 and *Prelude to Mars*, 1965.

Title change: *Master of Space.*
Lancer (US), 1961.

Title change: *The Space Dreamers.*
Lancer (US), 1969.

EARTHLIGHT

Sidgwick & Jackson (hd), 1954*; Pan, 1957.

In: *Across The Sea of Stars*, 1959, and *A Second Arthur Clarke Omnibus*, 1968.

REACH FOR TOMORROW (collection)

Ballantine (Us hd/paper), 1956; Gollancz (hd), 1962*; Corgi 1970.*

THE CITY AND THE STARS

(Expanded and rewritten version of *Against The Fall of Night*)

Harcourt (US), 1956; Huller (hd) 1956; Corgi, 1957*; Gollancz (hd), 1968*.

In: *From the Ocean, From the Stars*, 1962.

THE DEEP RANGE

Harcourt (US hd), 1957; Muller (hd), 1957; Science Fiction Book Club (hd), 1960; Gollancz (hd), 1968*; Pan, 1970*.

In: *From the Ocean, From the Stars*, 1962.

TALES FROM THE WHITE HART (collection)
  Ballantine (US), 1957; Sidgwick & Jackson (hd/paper), 1972*.

THE OTHER SIDE OF THE SKY (collection)
  Harcourt (US hd), 1958; Gollancz (hd), 1961*. Science Fiction Book Club (hd), 1962; Corgi, 1963*.
  In: *From the Ocean, From the Stars,* 1962.

ACROSS THE SEA OF STARS (collection)
  Harcourt (US), 1959.
  Contains: *Earthlight, Childhood's End* and short stories.

A FALL OF MOONDUST
  Harcourt (US hd), 1961; Gollancz (hd), 1961*; Science Fiction Book Club (hd), 1963; Pan, 1964*.
  In: *A Second Arthur Clarke Omnibus,* 1968.

FROM THE OCEAN, FROM THE STARS (collection)
  Harcourt (US hd), 1962.
  Contains: *The City and the Stars, The Deep Range* and *The Other Side of the Sky.*

TALES OF TEN WORLDS (collection)
  Harcourt (US hd), 1962; Gollancz (hd), 1963*; Science Fiction Book Club (hd), 1964; Pan, 1965; Corgi, 1971*.

DOLPHIN ISLAND
  Winston (US hd), 1963; Gollancz (hd), 1963*; Dragon (Panther), 1968; Piccolo, 1976*.

AN ARTHUR CLARKE OMNIBUS (collection)
  Sidgwick & Jackson (hd), 1965.
  Contains: *Childhood's End, Prelude to Space* and *Expedition to Earth.*

PRELUDE TO MARS (collection)
  Harcourt (US hd), 1965.
  Contains: *Sands of Mars, Prelude to Space* and short stories.

TIME PROBE (anthology edited by Arthur Clarke)
  Delacorte (US hd), 1967; Gollancz (hd), 1967.

NINE BILLION NAMES OF GOD (collection)
Harcourt (US hd), 1967.

2001: A SPACE ODYSSEY
(Based on the screenplay of the film by Stanley Kubrick
and Arthur Clarke.)
New American Library (US hd), 1968; Hutchinson (hd),
1968*; Arrow, 1968*.

A SECOND ARTHUR CLARKE OMNIBUS (collection)
Sidgwick & Jackson (hd), 1968.
Contains: *Sands of Mars, Earthlight* and *A Fall of Moon-
dust*.

THE LION OF COMARRE AND AGAINST THE FALL OF NIGHT
(collection)
Harcourt (US hd), 1968; Gollancz (hd), 1970*; Corgi,
1972*.

THREE FOR TOMORROW (anthology edited by Arthur Clarke)
Gollancz (hd), 1970*; Sphere, 1972*.

THE LOST WORLDS OF 2001 (collection)
Signet (US), 1972; Sidgwick & Jackson (hd/paper),
1972*.

THE WIND FROM THE SUN (collection)
Harcourt (US hd), 1972; Gollancz (hd), 1972*; Corgi,
1974*.

OF TIME AND STARS (collection)
Gollancz (hd), 1972*; Puffin, 1974*.

RENDEZVOUS WITH RAMA
Gollancz (hd), 1973*; Pan, 1974*.

THE BEST OF ARTHUR C. CLARKE: 1937–1972 (collection
edited by Angus Wells.) Sphere, 1973; Sidgwick & Jackson
(hd), 1973*.

THE BEST OF ARTHUR C. CLARKE: 1937–1955. Sphere,
1976*.

THE BEST OF ARTHUR C. CLARKE: 1956–1972. Sphere,
1977*.

IMPERIAL EARTH
Gollanz (hd), 1975*. Pan, 1977*.